M

Jim Horlock

GRENDEL PRESS

ISBN: 978-1-960534-24-8 (Paperback)
ISBN: B0DQHYMN4Y (Ebook)

Written by Jim Horlock
Edited by Kieran Judge
Cover art by Coversthatkill

Published by Grendel Press LLC
www.grendelpress.com

CONTENTS

For Red, who held this still while I carved.

For Billy and Stu, for Jason and Michael and Freddy, who got me started.

PUMPKINS AND PROPOSITIONS

I T WAS HOT AND stuffy inside the mask, but Edward supposed you couldn't have everything. He wasn't one to spoil a good evening's entertainment by complaining about the little things.

He put the knife down gently on the kitchen counter, then leant back to admire his work. He pursed his lips in thought and they kissed the inner surface of the mask. It was a strange thing to kiss the inside of one's own face, but that was the reality; the mask was as much him now as his own flesh and bone.

"Ten minutes, Mr Stitches."

He steepled his long, gloved fingers just beneath his chin as he considered the piece. Certainly not his best work but he was rather pushed for time.

Edward was all for experimentation. Pushing boundaries was what defined his career. It was one of the reasons it had taken them so long to catch him the first time. Every scene he left behind was different; different instruments, different methods, and different people.

He had to admit, however, that this particular experiment had been a mistake. Perhaps he'd simply been caught up in the atmosphere. It was Halloween after all. Edward loved that everyone dressed up as monsters and attempted to frighten each other. He was so rarely allowed to join in, that he'd gotten carried away.

Jack o'lanterns were a particular favourite. Encouraging people to be creative with sharp objects was a wonderful idea and he loved seeing all the fantastic carvings people made with such a simple template.

He was forced to admit, however, that pumpkins were certainly a better medium to work with than people.

How was a candle supposed to stay lit when she kept leaking everywhere? Maybe if he'd had time to dry her out...

He picked up the knife and turned from the kitchen. The apartment was small and open plan, so he could see the whole living room from where he stood.

The body was where he'd left it, throat precisely slit before the removal of the head. The blood splatter he'd left above the mantle had been every bit as spectacular as Edward had hoped, a cascade of reds to rival a Monet sunset. The body had stopped bleeding several minutes ago, and the awful brown carpet was now stained a deep red. It was a vast improvement.

The other victim was still in the bathroom where Edward had surprised her. She'd had no idea that her husband was already dead. He had smashed her skull in against the mirror. And then the sink. And then the toilet cistern. By that point the body was almost headless, so he'd dropped it onto the floor and arranged the mirror shards into a halo around the absent skull. Edward regretted his lack of time with glass — he'd always admired the work of Simon Berger — but whenever he got hold of a hammer, he got too distracted for such patient work.

"Five minutes, Mr Stitches," said a voice inside his mask.

Rawlins.

Edward rolled his shoulders and eased away some of the tension that voice placed on his neck. Edward was not an overly picky killer. Everyone was the same on the inside, as he'd repeatedly discovered. Still, some people deserved his attentions more than others, and he'd put Rawlins at the head of that category. The man was a miserable coward hiding behind borrowed authority and a gun, blunt and crass and smelling of stale cigarettes. Edward would love to find him in the dark one night, when his body armour was on the rack and his gun was far from hand.

Edward wandered idly to the window and peeped out through the blinds. It was against the rules, but rules were meant to be tested. He was content to bend them in little ways until he could free himself completely. These were petty rebellions one had to enjoy the little things.

Halloween meant there were people out in the streets, screaming and stuffing themselves with chocolate. Such a shame he was restricted to a single floor of a single building when he could contribute to the screaming. It was a waste of his talents.

The streetlight reflected dully off his mask, a smooth grey metal with black eyeholes but no nose. The mouth was leather string cross-stitched into a smile.

"Make your way to the extraction point, Mr Stitches.".

Edward picked up his plain black hold-all and made his way from Apartment 304, stepping lightly over the man he'd gutted in the hallway. They'd left bloody handprints on the wall where they'd tried to pull themselves along, weighed down by the anchor of their own intestines behind them, wet and heavy. Edward mused briefly over the composition they'd made.

"Bold but amateurish."

He reached the door to the fire exit and glanced fondly at the severed hands he'd pinned to the wall earlier with screwdrivers. Each was from a different victim. A message of togetherness. He hoped the police appreciated his efforts. Sighing, he stepped into the stairwell and left the floor behind. There were rules he had to follow and, while they chafed at him, they were preferable to a permanent set of handcuffs and the death penalty. He already escaped that once.

He climbed the stairs until he reached the door to the roof.

"You know the procedure," said the voice in his mask.

Edward removed his clothes and folded them neatly into a pile. The knife he left on top. It was a beautiful thing, ceramic and matte black, incredibly sharp. It had certainly been his favourite of all the items in tonight's bag of tricks, hence it was given the place of honour atop his clothes, rather than being relegated to the hold-all with the others, a little 'thank you' to the blade for a wonderful date. The drill had been fun, and the cleaver would always have a place in his heart (or someone's heart, anyway) but that knife was precise, elegant, and absolutely suited to his purpose. Edward considered it to be a perfect fit for him.

Once he was naked, barring the mask, he stretched his pale body, observing the way the lean muscles and tendons bunched beneath his skin. It often struck him as odd that he was made of meat just like everyone else when he felt like stainless steel inside.

The door to the roof opened to reveal several burly-looking men in body armour and visored helmets. "Control, this is Spectre Six," one of them said into his radio. "Proceeding with Extraction."

This was the part where Edward always entered into a private fantasy of escape. He could reach the first man in a heartbeat and jab his throat with stiff fingers. While the man choked to death on his collapsed throat, Edward would have time to seize the knife again and slash the neck of the next one. He could probably get about four of them before they gunned him down. Perhaps five.

As much as he hated his captors, they weren't stupid. Three guards always stood by the helicopter, ready to open fire if he made any sudden moves, regardless of their comrades being in the way. He'd never get to them in time.

And if he were to head back down the stairwell? Well, the bomb in his mask would take care of that.

The men had their faces completely covered, but Edward knew Rawlins would be one of those by the helicopter. Even with a gun, he was too much of a coward to get close. He always watched from a safe distance, ready for any excuse to pull the trigger.

So, just as he had done previously, Edward submitted to having his hands cuffed behind his back and being forced out onto the roof. He didn't care that he was naked in front of these men. The indignity was theirs, not his. There was, however, a chill wind in the air, and Edward's skin goose-bumped instantly. He suppressed a shiver.

"All set?" asked one of the men as they reached the helicopter.

"Spectre Three haven't checked in," grunted one of the helicopter men. Rawlins.

"Mr Beast is a handful," said Edward. "I hear he has to be sedated every time, the poor thing."

Edward felt the man behind him freeze.

Newbie.

Despite Spectre operatives all wearing visors, Edward had learned to tell this latest batch apart. Johnson was the tallest, easily a head over the others. Antoine stuffed his shoes to seem taller; you could hear it in his footsteps. Michaelsen always wore the same cologne, and Davies smelled of cheap whiskey. Edward liked to make it clear he knew who was who, despite the attempts at anonymity.

"How did he know Mr Beast was out?"

Edward turned his head, one of the dark eye holes facing the man over his shoulder. "Have you met the man? I haven't, but he carries quite a formidable stench."

"You can't smell him from here." His voice wavered. "No fucking way."

Excellent.

Fear led to panic and panic made people clumsy. Often fatally so, in Edward's experience.

"Shut it, Kent," said Rawlins. "Don't engage the Mask in conversation, just get him onboard!"

Edward smiled. It didn't matter what Rawlins said now, Kent would talk. By the end of tomorrow, there would be rumours flying around that Mr Stitches had superhuman senses.

In reality, he'd simply stolen a glance at the prisoner manifest before they'd bundled him onto the helicopter. It was amazing how people would rather believe in the supernatural than simplicity.

Rawlins jabbed the butt of his gun into Edward's kidney, who let out a hiss of pain through clenched teeth. "You're not here to talk," Rawlins snarled. "You're just here to do the dirty work."

Edward smelled tobacco through the mints he sucked to try and cover the smell. He straightened back up and considered several options of verbal riposte. Before he made a decision, the clatter of gunfire and a savage howling interrupted him.

"Oh dear," he said. "It appears Mr Beast is being uncooperative."

"Get in!"

Edward stepped into the helicopter, which always smelled of oil and disinfectant, and sat in his allocated seat. He allowed himself to be locked in with numerous straps and chains, taking some satisfaction in the panicked radio calls.

"Spectre Three, what is your status?"

Silence.

"Spectre Three, respond! Can you hear me?"

"God-fucking-dammit, Spectre Three, respond!"

Edward leant back and made himself comfortable for the flight home.

He had no idea where the facility actually was. The flight took different lengths of time, even in the same return journey, and he suspected that this was intentional, taking a longer route to throw off any attempt to guess the facility's location. He'd once caught a glimpse outside the helicopter just before it landed and saw the area was heavily forested and remote, which made sense. The last place you'd want a concrete hive of convicted killers was right beside a population centre. Even his transit from the aircraft after arrival gave few clues since the helicopter pad was on a giant lift mechanism, lowering it inside the facility before allowing anyone to disembark.

On arrival they took him out, still blindfolded, and marched him through the facility. The corridors back to his cell were plain concrete, with no windows or distinguishing markings, though that hadn't stopped him memorizing the way.

The men were still unsettled as they escorted him to his room. Evidently there had still been no response from Spectre Three. Edward smiled.

How interesting.

He wondered how many Mr Beast had killed. Enough for them to risk detonating his mask? Or had they managed to gun him down? Edward had no respect for Mr Beast, who was reportedly little more than a howling lunatic, but he envied him the kills. Edward hadn't murdered a guard in months.

His cell was relatively plain, though he had been allowed a carpet. He used to have books, but he'd crushed a guard's throat with one eight months ago, so they'd taken them away. He still hadn't decided whether it was worth it. Then again, the guard had been very rude. The cell itself was circular, concrete walls stretching twelve feet high and topped with a metal dome. The dome was rigged with powerful spotlights which they turned on when they wanted to deny him sleep. It was safe to assume there were cameras up there, too. That was only logical.

Edward was not allowed coat-hangers for reasons that he considered to be unfair, so he placed his neatly folded clothes along one wall. In the opposite corner was the shower and toilet. No curtain, of course. There was nowhere to hide in the cell. Even the bed was just a mattress on the floor with no space beneath to play bogeyman. They'd even neglected to give him a spring one, with delightful metal parts inside that he could use on lonely, inventive evenings.

Edward showered quickly. The water was cold and drummed against the outside of his mask. They would be along soon to remove it, but he didn't want to wait to shower. He didn't enjoy sweatiness.

Afterwards he paced back and forth for a while, letting the droplets fall from his pale body. He wasn't allowed towels, but he didn't mind that so much. His footsteps made no sound on the carpet, despite its thinness.

Once he was sufficiently dry, he put on a grey bathrobe. It was threadbare and old, devoid of even a belt. It was Dr Liebling's little game to approve Edward's requests for items but fail to produce them in any kind of quality. Edward understood the need to remove anything that could be used as a weapon, he actually took it as a compliment, but serving tea in a Styrofoam cup was barbaric. Edward refused to give them the satisfaction of complaining. Instead, he spent his time with Liebling fantasizing about how he was going to kill the man.

He listened near the door. No footsteps. Odd. Liebling always insisted on an interview whilst Edward was still 'fresh' from the field. He never arrived later than twenty minutes after Edward got back to his cell.

Perhaps Mr Beast's extracurricular activities were keeping the psychological staff busy.

A FULL HOUR LATER, when Dr Liebling finally arrived, he looked dishevelled. His greying fringe was damp and his glasses were slightly askew. Edward watched his rapid blinking, his constant face-touching and lip-licking, and savoured it all. This was supposed to be the good doctor's place of power, supreme in his confidence and his conceit. Edward intended to instruct him at length on the frailty of his imagined control, but until such a time as that was possible, it was pleasing to see Liebling concerned.

With Dr Liebling, as always, were his prime henchmen. Their real names were Michaels and Jameson, but Edward referred to them as Thing 1 and Thing 2. Both were huge, broad-shouldered and broad faced, with heavy brows and sinewy necks. Edward wondered vaguely how many strokes of a hacksaw it would take to decapitate them.

Thing 1 caught him around the neck with the control pole without so much as a hello. The wire tightened and the thug twisted the pole upwards, forcing Edward onto his tiptoes. While he fought for breath, Thing 2 bound his hands and feet together, then they forced him onto his knees with more aggression than necessary. Ordinarily this was accompanied by smug looks from the doctor, but today he just looked old and worried.

With Edward fully restrained, they entered the combination at the back of his mask. He listened to the clicking, like clockwork in his head, and when the metal came away he took a deep breath. The air in the prison was always stale with a clinical edge, and he'd considered the possibility that it was drugged, but it seemed unlikely. The staff wore no breathing apparatus. Maybe the tang in the air came from industrial cleaners.

Now free, he tilted his head from side to side. Strands of brown hair fell into his eyes. It was longer than he'd like; they hadn't worked out how to cut it without casualties yet.

Thing 2 removed the arm and leg restraints, two sets of cuffs with a solid bar between them – a portable hogtying device, essentially. Thing 1 grudgingly removed the control pole from Edward's neck. He stood, careful to show an air of nonchalance with his expression.

"Doctor," he greeted Liebling. "You look terrible."

"Mr Stitches. Please have a seat."

Thing 1 kept an eye on Edward, his hand twitching near the taser at his belt, while Thing 2 brought a chair in for the doctor. Edward, as always, was made to sit on the floor. Yet another way Liebling pettily displayed his power. Edward crossed his legs and kept his vaguely amused smile to show he didn't care in the least. Inside the comfort of his mind, he imagined breaking both of Liebling's ankles before forcing him to run through the woods. The thought helped him maintain his calm.

The doctor shuffled the papers on his clipboard.

"Oh dear," Edward remarked. "Mr Beast really has shaken you up, hasn't he?"

Dr Liebling glared at him through round spectacles, Edward's mockery giving the doctor some steel back in his spine. He was still tense, but was determined to control himself in front of his prisoner.

"Did you learn anything in the field today?"

Edward considered this briefly.

"A human head does not an adequate jack o'lantern make," he offered sagely.

The doctor sighed, a frustrated teacher dealing with a disruptive pupil. "Your attempts to shock me are wasted, Edward," he cautioned. "You think your acts are the worst I've seen?"

"That depends on who else you have in here." Edward gestured around him, trying to bait the doctor. He was ever eager to learn more about the other infamous killers that had ended up in the Mask Program instead of meeting their maker. He had a few code names; Mr Beast, Miss Malice, Mr Monster, but so far that was all. Knowledge was power, and the more he learnt about the facility and its personnel, the more likely his chances of escape.

He also knew that Liebling would deny him anything he wanted simply because he could, so he had to be careful not to register too much interest.

"You have never raped your victims, Edward."

He waved a hand dismissively. "The exchange of bodily fluids does not interest me."

"You don't cannibalise them either."

"I tried it once out of curiosity. I couldn't see what all the fuss was about. No different than any other meat, really."

"Rape and cannibalism are often displays of dominance," Liebling stated. "But you don't seem driven to dominate your victims. You torture them but it wouldn't be fair to say you are cruel. A cruel man derives pleasure from the pain of others, but with you, it's not their pain which gives your pleasure. Tell me, Edward, why do you display them? At each of your crime scenes, on each of your deployments for us, you displayed at least one, usually more. And we all know about the project which got you caught in the first place."

Edward shrugged, refusing to rise to the bait. The mention of his capture was clearly intended to spark a reaction, but pompous psychobabble meant nothing to him. He let the little man ramble on because he couldn't physically stop him. Yet.

The doctor had aged horribly during Edward's time at the facility. His hairline receded at a rapid rate of knots and the strands that survived this culling were greying. Every time Edward saw the man he seemed to have gained a decade. He supposed it must be a stress of the job. He sincerely hoped it didn't kill Liebling before he'd had a chance to himself.

"I think you display them because you're trying to impress someone. Father figure left you at a young age? Or maybe mother didn't pay you enough attention. You're desperate for approval. You're always reluctant to talk about your early life. Tell me; what do you remember of your childhood?"

Edward resisted the urge to roll his eyes. This was a common thread the doctor pulled at.

Liebling studied him intently. "There are other ways to win approval," he said after a few moments. "Ways in which you might be rewarded."

This is new.

Edward steadied himself, tried not to show his piqued interest. The doctor had never attempted a reward system with Edward before. The reluctance with which it was offered suggested that it wasn't his idea. Someone else's order, then. But who gave it?

"You've been with us for almost two years. In that time, you've had a dozen deployments. You have killed or grievously wounded a dozen personnel at this facility, but never tried to escape. Not out in the field, and not from here. Why?"

"Perhaps I'm biding my time."

"Perhaps," the doctor agreed. "I'm certainly inclined to think so. You're not a stupid man. You know we can detonate your mask at any time. You don't have a way to bypass the security systems, and you don't know where to go. But there are others who see your compliance as, if not good behaviour, then at least an acceptance of the rules that have been set."

Edward couldn't help it. His eyes narrowed slightly in annoyance. It bothered him to be thought of as compliant and submissive. He had no idea what the true nature of the facility was, but its regular deployment of masked murderers into the field – a field filled with unarmed civilians, no less – had suited his purpose. He avoided the death sentence and he got to continue to be creative. Perhaps he'd allowed himself to grow too comfortable. He wasn't some wild animal to be kept on a leash, slowly fed scraps until begging was second nature. He was not to be domesticated.

On the other hand, his present choices were limited. What option did he have but to follow the orders of the men who strapped high explosives to his face every time he left his cell?

Kill them, of course.

"I can see you thinking, Edward," said Liebling, smugly. "We both know what you're going to ask, so go ahead and ask it."

Edward exercised considerable restraint in not lunging for the doctor. Thing 1's fingers twitched. "You're the one angling towards a point, doctor," Edward said. "Will you be arriving at it before your decaying health consumes you?"

Liebling's lip twitched, a micro-expression of irritation. That was not the response he wanted.

One point to me.

"There are those who believe you might be of some use to us as something other than a blunt instrument or a lab rat," said Liebling, putting emphasis on the word 'blunt'. It implied thuggery. A lack of finesse. He knew Edward would be insulted. "Personally, I couldn't disagree with them more, but they want to meet with you despite my recommendation."

"A job interview?" Edward arched an eyebrow. "Why, are they so eager to replace you?"

A cheap barb, he knew, but he'd been unable to resist. Liebling didn't take the bait.

One point to him.

"They'll be here in a few hours." He stood up and Thing 2 collected the chair. "At which point they will evaluate the exact level of your compliance. Tell me, do you know who else we keep here? Who they were before?"

Edward said nothing. He had no intention of revealing the extent of his knowledge to Liebling.

"The worst of the worst. That's who we have. We've collected some of the most violent, disturbed and gruesome killers mankind has ever produced. Your quest for approval is in vain. Compared to them, you are not remotely frightening. You're a small fish in a big pond. The real reason you were chosen over the others isn't because you're impressive, but because you pose so little threat."

Liebling's insults echoed around Edward's head long after the man had left the cell. Edward paced back and forth, bare feet padding silently across the cold hard floor.

Two-one to Liebling. Unfortunate.

Tempting as it was to lose himself in vivid daydreams of bloody revenge, Edward forced himself to focus. It was true that he hadn't yet attempted escape from this facility. Each failure would only reduce the chances of future success, and Edward had no desire to make things any more difficult for himself. He had convinced himself it was best to wait until he had more information but, so far, he had garnered nothing of use.

Perhaps it would be opportunity, not information, that would be the key to his escape. Edward decided to hear what these mysterious authorities wanted.

T HEY WERE MILITARY, THAT much was clear from the sound of their boots. Heavy footed and unconsciously in step, like a Spectre Team. Edward counted six of them despite the echoes. He smiled in satisfaction when the cell door opened and six men entered.

They fanned out, backs to the wall, keeping their distance. His smile widened. These men feared him, despite their guns; he read the nervousness in their body language.

Good.

Well, five of them. Their leader, broad-shouldered and grey-haired, a nasty scar making his lips into a permanent snarl, showed no evidence of nerves. Small, glinting eyes scrutinised Edward, as though he was an unusual breed of deer to be considered before shooting, stuffing, and mounting.

Edward held the gaze and kept his smile.

"How many people have you killed, son?" the man grunted. His voice was like lumber mills and whiskey.

Edward considered the question. "Do you know, I have no idea. It never occurred to me to count. How many have you killed?"

The man ignored the question. "You have friends in here?" His voice could rear horses and chew its own tobacco.

"I don't believe I've ever had a friend. I don't particularly feel the need for them."

The man regarded him for another few slow seconds. "My name is Colonel Tucker Marsden," he said. "I run the security here. The boys here belong to me. Hand-picked by me and trained by me. Now, I don't involve myself in the science or the psychiatry that goes on here. My only concern is containment, and in that, I have a problem."

"You refer, I assume, to Mr Beast's current jaunt."

Psychiatry or the science? What "science" is that if it's independent from psychiatry?

"We have confined him to an area, but I am faced with a shortage of men," said the colonel. "Can't leave this place unguarded. Can't take men off the perimeter in case he slips through. The men I would have used to take him down he's already slaughtered, and my closest reinforcements are still hours away."

"So trigger the bomb in his mask and scrape him into a bag."

"Not an option."

Not an option? Interesting. So, the bomb either became disabled by accident or they're refusing to detonate it for some other reason.

"That's where you come in," said the colonel.

Edward raised an eyebrow.

"You're going in in to bring back Mr Beast," said the colonel. "One killer after another."

DESIGNATION: SUBJECT 11

Alias: Mr Cadaver

Subject Class: Prometheus

Lead Physician: Dr Aiden

Description: Journal entry provided by subject at Dr Aiden's request.

It was the neck wound that gave her away.

Pinched skin, abrasions, bruising. From a rope. I knew right away she'd been hanged. Or maybe she'd hanged herself, you know? Either way, you couldn't miss the death-wound. It was almost beautiful. Deep purples, harsh reds and bright pinks. Kinda like a sunset. She didn't even wear a scarf to hide it. I guess she felt safe, knowing no one could see it. She didn't know I could. I'm the only one that can.

For a long time, I didn't realise I was special. I thought everyone was crazy, you know? Letting the living dead walk amongst them. Sitting on the bus next to a guy with his face all blown off by a shotgun blast like it's normal. I once saw a little girl with her scalp missing playing jump-rope with her friends in the park. They were laughing and singing songs with this scalpless monster right there. Makes me think of that movie, you know? Where the guy puts on the glasses and he can see all the aliens but no one else can. Except I wasn't wearing glasses.

I was never a bright kid. School was hard for me. I tried, I really did, but he just didn't understand missing numbers and I've got no head for remembering stuff, you know? It didn't bother me much, even when the other kids made fun, but my Ma, she was upset. She wanted me to do well.

I remember her crying at parent/teacher night.

"He has the mind," the teachers told her. "He can do it. He just can't seem to apply himself. He just isn't interested."

I knew they were just being kind for her sake. The truth was I didn't have the mind. Things wouldn't stay in my head. I was sorry I'd made his mother cry, but I couldn't make myself different.

She was still crying on the way home.

She said to me: "I'm not angry with you, honey. I just want what's best for you. I want you to have a future. I want you to find something that you can apply yourself to. I know you will. We can't give up hope."

She leaned over to give me a kiss on the cheek.

Then the truck hit us.

Found out later that the driver had fallen asleep at the wheel. By the time I woke up from the coma, Ma was gone. I was all alone in the world. The doctors said brain damage. No money, no home, no family, and brain damage. It was a pretty dark time for me.

That's when I started to see the living dead.

I followed her for a few days first. That's crucial. It's important to study them. Gotta learn where they live, where they work, if they had friends or people who might try to protect them.

Don't be seen. Find out when they'll be alone.

This one worked as a lunch lady at a school. That was unsanitary. Ma had hated germs. This monster had to go, before she got the kids ill.

It wasn't difficult. She lived alone in a small bungalow in a quiet neighbourhood not far from the school. No security light. No alarm system. No deadbolts on the doors. What do the living dead have to fear, you know?

I found the rope in the garden shed. It was perfect. The visions were never wrong. See, you gotta kill the living dead the same way they died the first time. It's the only way. I did the guy on the bus with a shotgun, and I scalped the little girl from the park. Little Miss Lunch-Lady died by the rope. That's the key. The visions just show me how to do it.

I had to break the back window to get in. The glass made a little noise but didn't wake her. She had a dog; I'd seen her walking it while I was scoping her out. Lucky for me the vision works on animals. I saw a cleaver-hole in its skull, so I knew to bring one with me. It fit perfectly.

I got the rope around her neck while she lay face down asleep on the bed. The noose tightened before she could cry out. Then I stood above her and planted my foot on her back. A couple minutes pulling on that rope, and it was all done. One more monster killed.

The last part is always checking the death-wound, so I rolled her over. It was a perfect match, just like when I'd first seen her.

I'm applying myself just like Ma wanted. I think she'd be proud.

A Night on the Town

T HE BLINDFOLD DIDN'T STOP Edward
from knowing they'd brought him to a
part of the facility he'd never been to before. The
air smelled different, less chemical, and there was
some quality to it that made him think they were
deeper underground.

They took no chances. He was wheeled,
Hannibal Lecter-style, on an upright gurney
rather than being allowed to walk, and his
mask was back in place. Obviously Liebling's
insults earlier had been meant to put Edward off
accepting whatever offer these men had for him.
Edward savoured the look on his face as they
removed the blindfold.

There was a mass of screens at the far end of
the room. One showed footage from a helicopter

circling a city block, another the view from the top of a building. Only when it panned left and revealed a pair of hands on a high-powered rifle did Edward realise it was a helmet-mounted camera. A third live-stream was a news station. A pretty blonde reporter on the scene shouted into her microphone. Several buildings were ablaze behind her.

"You set the city on fire?" Edward's tone was one of both mild surprise and approval.

"Gives us good reason to evacuate the civilian population," the colonel said. "An excuse to have a presence and establish a cordon. Plus, it gives us plenty of cover for the operation."

"Mr Beast is afraid of fire, so the flames should keep him from attempting to the leave the area," Dr Liebling added.

"He told you that, doctor?" asked Edward, bemused.

"Mr Beast doesn't speak. But we have access to various files on him. I've been ordered to share them with you in order for you to establish a profile."

His tone suggested that he was anything but happy about this. Edward couldn't have cared less about the psychological profile of that raving lunatic, but he would certainly look at the files if it upset Liebling.

"I'm curious, colonel," said Edward, pointedly not addressing his questions towards Liebling. "How was Mr Beast able to overpower so many of your highly trained and heavily armed men?"

Liebling stiffened.

"He is a dangerous man." The colonel's face locked up like a bank vault door.

"Aren't we all, colonel? But I doubt I would have been able to overcome the entirety of Spectre Three."

Liebling tried to draw the attention back to himself. "As I told you, Edward. You are not the most formidable individual in the Program."

"If I need your professional opinion, doctor, I'll ask for it." The colonel turned back to Edward. "You've been selected for a number of reasons. Your compliance is one of them, but we're also relying on your capability. We need Mr Beast brought down. Alive if possible, but I'm just as happy with dead. You capable of that, Mr Stitches?"

A number of scientists in the room started to protest, but the colonel shot them a warning look and they scattered like a school of fish in the presence of the shark.

The speech was probably supposed to be rousing, but Edward been distracted by the presence of the emergency fire axe on the wall and had missed half of it due to the ensuing fantasy. "Oh, I'm sure I'll manage. I'd salute you, but you know…" He wriggled his arms in the restraints. "I don't suppose you'd care to loosen them?"

"You will remain restrained until you enter the field, as per normal procedure. Spectre Six will drop you in."

"How comforting to be amongst friends," said Edward dryly. "So, what tools will I be taking on this little jaunt?"

"No firearms," the colonel said instantly.

"Never liked them anyway."

"You'll be supplied with a standard toolkit, as per routine Ops."

"Nothing special?"

The colonel narrowed his eyes beneath bushy brows. "What did you have in mind?" he said.

Behind his mask, Edward grinned.

THE HELICOPTER RIDE WAS more pleasant than usual, at least as far as Edward was concerned. Rawlins did not share his enthusiasm. Strapped in closest to the rear cargo door, as comfortable a distance as he was likely to get in the close confines of the helicopter, Rawlins seethed.

"I don't understand," said Kent the Newbie. "Why are we going out again? Twice in one night? That's weird, right?"

"Doesn't matter," rumbled Johnson. "Colonel says jump."

"Put two and two together," said Michaelsen, his tone suggesting that he was rolling his eyes behind that plexiglass visor. "Spectre Three are down. Mr Beast is still loose."

"They're sending *him*?" Kent jerked a thumb at Edward.

"Exciting, isn't it?" said Edward. "Relax, Kent, I'm confident that some of you will make it out of this experience alive."

"He knows my name!" Kent panicked, shrinking back as far from Edward as his seat would allow. "How the fuck does he know my name?"

"Stow it!" Rawlins spat. "Do not engage the Mask. Your only concern is your objectives."

"I bet you're fun at parties," Edward remarked.

Edward couldn't read Rawlins's expression through the visor, but he could guess it was utter loathing. He wondered vaguely why the man hated him so much before deciding that he didn't care.

T HEY REACHED THE CITY in record time.
      Edward supposed taking the scenic route
in the name of obfuscation wasn't an option.
He didn't care; any excuse to get back out.

Before his capture, Edward had selected his
targets based on his mood at the time and
their availability. Given the opportunity, he
would have killed everyone he passed by, but he
had been realistic and cautious when necessary.
Now he just killed whatever was put in front of
him.

The analogy about scraps and begging for
them came to his mind again but he put it aside.
There were opportunities to be exploited here.

What a treat to hunt a fellow Mask.

The helicopter put him down on a rooftop as
usual.

Rawlins turned to him. "We will monitor you
from here. If I see anything I don't like, I'll
trigger that detonator and turn your head into
a fine red mist."

"Let's hope you don't happen across any
mirrors," said Edward.

His clothes and kit bag were placed just inside the rooftop access door before Spectre Six retreated to their helicopter and released him, naked and masked, to go about his work.

He dressed quickly, pleased that his regular plain grey suit had been cleaned between deployments, and checked the contents of the kit bag. Content, he slung it over his shoulder and made his way down the stairs, whistling cheerfully to himself.

"A reminder, Mr Stitches," said a voice in his head. Not Rawlins this time, but the colonel. "No witnesses. We cannot have any evidence of you, or Mr Beast, left behind. You are sanctioned to use lethal force."

It had never occurred to him to use any other kind of force.

Disappointingly, he didn't meet any witnesses on his way out of the building.

Edward hadn't set foot on a street in years. Looking up at the buildings sent a ripple of vertigo through him. The apartment buildings seemed to sprawl overhead. They towered, leaning over the street, squared teeth of steel and concrete, biting down on the sky. He frowned.

The cities he remembered never looked like this.

Edward wondered what part of the world he was in. Wherever it was, the population must be teeming. He thought about the buildings he'd been inside since they first strapped the metal to his face. Had they all been this large? He had only ever been set loose on one or two floors at a time and, of course, wasn't allowed near the windows.

He felt suddenly at odds with the world, disconnected, as though his version of reality no longer matched what was in front of him. Was this what madness felt like?

He shook himself.

This isn't the time.

Mr Beast was a dangerous individual. The footage Edward had looked at before his deployment only cemented his opinion that Mr Beast was a complete savage, utterly brutal in the execution of anyone he got his hands on. It seemed doubtful he would feel any kinship towards Edward, despite their overlapping interests, nor give him anything but his full, murderous attention.

"Mr Stitches," the colonel's voice again. "The building at your two o'clock."

Edward rolled his eyes. "If you're going to talk through this whole thing, I'm going to struggle to enjoy it," he said.

"We're not here for your enjoyment, Mr Stitches."

"Spoilsport."

Edward crossed the street and made for the building. The stink of smoke was heavy in the air and the fire several streets away burned against the night. He heard sirens and, if he strained his ears, distant screaming.

It was delightful.

M R BEAST'S WORK WAS every bit as crude as Edward had expected, but he was surprised to find some appreciation for it. The sheer violence was undeniable. Skulls had been smashed, throats crushed, and limbs torn from their sockets. Mr Beast had ripped through the people in the lobby like they were made of paper. His strength seemed almost beyond human.

The files mentioned that the procedure for Mr Beast was different to that of the other Masks. After all, there wasn't much to be gained from explaining to an animal that you could blow up his head with the touch of a button. Bargains and reasoning were not an option. Instead, Mr Beast's mask was fitted with an additional device, a kind of sonic emitter that shrieked in his ears when triggered. It was used as a deterrent whenever Mr Beast threatened to stray into an area outside the mission boundary. The short sharp screech of feedback would send him scurrying back the other way. His cell at the facility was fitted with similar technology to keep him from battering himself to death against the walls.

Edward wondered what other tactics of coercion were used against the Masks. How long was his leash compared to others?

As he pressed on, he felt a familiar cold sensation slip across his skin and it sent a pleasant shudder down his spine. His senses sharpened. The sound of his footsteps faded as muscle memory adjusted his gait for stealth. It always started like this when he committed to a kill, predator instincts that should have been long left behind with some reptilian ancestor awakening at the prospect of blood. This was the feeling of stalking, of hunting the prey.

Edward made his way up the stairs, following the carnage Mr Beast left behind.

The block looked like any of the others that Edward had visited: dozens of small apartments crammed in together behind thin doors and between thin walls. The stillness of death was on the place, that feeling somewhere got when all the living had left. The first few floors were empty, presumably evacuated. Much like Edward, Mr Beast had only been let loose in the upper areas of the building.

Edward took the time to wonder at the purpose of the Program. Why were the Masks released to kill in these areas? Who decided the parameters? It was a mystery with frustratingly few clues, and he shelved his thoughts quickly after each consideration to focus on the task at hand.

It didn't take Edward long to find the next sign of Mr Beast. A man lay dead, his torso little more than a sack of pulp, bones gravelled by savage blows. He'd thrown up a lot of blood before he died, drowning on his own fluids. Holes had been punched in the corridor walls, missed strikes at a target or possibly just anger venting itself through random violent action. Either way, Edward noted the size of the holes.

"The beast has big paws," he said to himself.

The next victim he found was jawless, his tongue flopped out on his neck like an old sock. Edward tracked the missing mandible by the delightful arc of blood on the wall to its resting place several feet away. It had seemingly been torn free by hand and flung aside. Once more, he marvelled at the strength of Mr Beast. It didn't seem possible that a man, who was in his late fifties according to his file, could be capable of such ferocious power.

What aren't I being told? Is this why they won't detonate his mask?

The rest of that floor was much the same, bodies torn apart or pounded into oblivion, doors ripped free from hinges, furniture hurled from the path of fury. Edward found one woman who had been crushed rather messily when her refrigerator had been thrown across the room. The large bloody footprints of Mr Beast made a path through the carnage.

Edward took in these details with the attitude of a critic at an art exhibition. He mulled over them, inspected them, occasionally moved around to study them from a different angle. His approach was unhurried, a curious meander through corridors of violent endings.

Three floors later, Edward found a member of Spectre Three.

He was surrounded by casings from useless gunshots. The weapon lay beneath the man's dangling feet, and he was pinned to the wall by some twisted piece of metal through his neck. Edward guessed it was a chair leg. The metal was jagged, ripped clean from the furniture by hand.

"A most violent perforation," Edward mused. "I'm reminded of Vermiglio's *Jael and Sisera*. Congratulations to you, sir, to have been made into something approaching beauty."

The dead man did not reply.

It gave Edwards a warm feeling to see a member of one of the Spectre Teams so brutally executed, if only because they all looked the same and he could picture it as Rawlins.

The next two Spectre men had been smashed together so hard that their helmets and the heads inside had become an indecipherable puzzle of flesh, bone and plastic. Edward crouched for a moment and considered it. "OK," he admitted, "I like this one. Avantgarde. Bold. Expressive. Perhaps Mr Beast has the soul of an artist beneath his muscle."

"Those were my men, Mr Stitches." The colonel's voice was close to a growl.

"They're not anymore, colonel. Now, they're far more interesting."

He noted even more spent casings littering the floor. Edward was no expert on ballistics, but he had seen a lot of blood spatter in his time and saw no sign of exit wound spray in the corridor. Either Mr Beast was either walking around with a lot of lead inside him, or the Spectres had managed to miss every shot.

Edward stepped over the bodies and continued his investigation.

The window at the end of the hall had been smashed outwards, as though a large gorilla had propelled itself through it. Edward didn't go there immediately. Instead, he paused at an open door to one of the apartments where another Spectre lay dead.

This one had been shot.

The Masks were not allowed guns, so the Spectre Teams were not typically outfitted with bulletproof equipment. Most of their gear was designed to mitigate stabbing, slicing, or bludgeoning. With no protection, the gunshots had ploughed straight through the armour and into the man's chest. Four shots in a tight grouping.

The door to the apartment had been smashed off its hinges. Almost certainly the work of Mr Beast. The neat marksmanship was absolutely the work of someone else.

Edward stepped over the threshold.

The apartment was small, as he'd expected, but neat and clean, save for the blood-stained footprints of Mr Beast. There were few unnecessary items, no decorations or ornaments. The kitchen was spotless and, if the cupboards was anything to go by, hardly used. He found coffee, a few tins of food, and very little else.

The first real clues came from the bedroom. The bed was immaculately made, and Edward was not surprised to find, when he slid open the drawers of the chest, that each item of clothing was neatly folded.

A man's clothes. A single chair and a single bed. A very neat man who lived alone.

"Colonel, whose apartment is this? And what regiment did he serve in?"

"You think they were military?"

"Oh yes, I'd say so."

"Our people are checking the list of residents now. Is this relevant?"

Edward got on his knees and checked under the bed. He pulled a box from its hiding place and removed the lid. Frozen faces stared up at him from photographs inside.

"If I had to guess, I'd say Mr Beast's rampage ended here. He entered the building from the roof, slaughtered his way down the stairs until the buzzing in his mask forced him to turn back on himself, at which point he rampaged his way back up again until he got here. He certainly forced his way into this apartment, but there's no body."

"So, the occupant wasn't in?"

"Well, if that was the case, the occupant wouldn't have been able to shoot one of your Spectre boys dead. Now hush, I'm thinking."

"He what?!"

"Hush." Edward pressed a finger to the stitched lips of his mask even though there was no-one to see it. "Thinking."

An awful, ragged howling sounded nearby, perhaps a block or two away. Gunfire followed.

"No time to think, Mr Stitches. Get moving before I change my mind about this whole deal."

With a disappointed sigh Edward replaced the photos with deliberate lethargy and put the box back in its hiding place. He picked up his kitbag again and left the apartment and its mysteries.

T HE SMASHED WINDOW LED to a fire escape down into a narrow alley. The building opposite was close enough for Edward to reach out and caress its brickwork. He looked up at the narrow strip of sky, but the glare of the lights meant he could see nothing. The scale threatened to topple him, and momentary vertigo caused the buildings to wave back and forth like seaweed in the tide.

Edward shook himself and descended. The city's strangeness was a mystery for another time.

He dropped into the alley from the lowest level of the metal staircase, landing in a crouch. He smelled blood. Mr Beast must have been caked in it. Edward felt his pulse quicken a little, the thrill of hunting in his veins. His excursions as a Mask hadn't involved this side of the art of the kill. He was simply unleashed on several floors of a building somewhere before being whisked away again. There was no need to track a target, to observe, to come close to them and wait for the opportunity. He hadn't realised how much he missed it.

He stole along the alleyway, a grey shadow, the feel of the air conjuring memories of other alleys on other nights. Of blood, of screams and sudden silences.

This street, just like the other, was deserted and quiet but for distant sirens and the crackle of flames. Broken glass crunched under foot from the shattered window of a looted electronics store. The remaining screen inside showed helicopter footage of the fire, which had already consumed several apartment blocks and was rapidly spreading. A perfect cover for the trail of bodies Mr Beast left behind. Edward hadn't really considered before how the facility got away with their routine deployment of the Masks before now. Over time they must have racked up quite the body count. Didn't anyone care that so many people were turning up dead?

Another mystery with no immediate answer. Edward turned from the screen and made his way north towards the noise he'd heard earlier.

Able to look properly around, Edward realised how alien the streets were to him. Glowing billboards projected advertisements in a three-dimensional light show like something from science fiction, and he didn't recognise the products advertised. If it weren't that the adverts were in English, Edward would have guessed he were somewhere futuristic, perhaps Tokyo or Dubai. It was certainly a far cry from the technology he remembered.

E DWARD GUESSED HE WAS around five minutes late to the scene.

Mr Beast was gone but, as before, he'd left behind a mess behind. Two police officers, one with his guts forcibly removed and cradled in his arms like a newborn, the other numbly staring into space, the first man's head in his lap.

"Good evening, officer," Edward said, brightly.

The surviving cop slowly turned his head towards Edward. He was pale and hardly blinking. His mouth moved a little, but no sound came out.

"It is a lovely evening," Edward replied. "I don't suppose you happen to have seen a large, angry, masked man come this way? Probably covered in blood and possibly in the company of a military-looking gentleman."

The officer frowned and looked down at his dead friend. Then he raised an arm and pointed to the entrance to the underground further down the street. The gates and boards that prohibited access had been splinted and thrown aside.

"M-mask," the officer croaked. His eyes were out of focus, irises adjusting and re-adjusting like little blue camera lenses.

"Mask," Edward agreed before burying a cleaver in his forehead. "Yes, indeed."

THE ABANDONED TRAIN STATION was every bit as dusty as Edward has expected it would be, but at least it made following the trail easier.

"Two pairs of footprints, colonel," Edward noted. "Mr Beast has made a friend, after all."

"We've found out who it is," the colonel replied. "Captain James Arkridge. Discharged due to injury after several tours overseas, decades ago."

"And what is it about the captain that makes him Beast-proof?"

The colonel cleared his throat awkwardly. "Mr Beast has a military background. We're still checking through the files, but it's possible that Arkridge and he knew each other."

"A reunion, then. A chance meeting of two former comrades in arms. The stirring of old feelings, the remembrance of an unbreakable bond."

"Could be."

"Oh, colonel, how unfortunate for you. The white coats must be kicking themselves."

"This isn't a laughing matter, Stitches. My men are dead."

"Perhaps you shouldn't have been so careless with them. Cheer up, there are always more men. And women, actually. I always thought it sexist that the security staff at the facility are predominantly male."

"Get on with it before I lose my patience and push this button."

"Temper, temper."

Edward followed the prints through the dust and down onto the tracks. The tunnel was large and dark, but he could see well enough to walk without tripping. Somewhere ahead in the darkness, he thought he caught the murmur of voices.

Carefully, he unzipped his kitbag again, grinning at the prospect of more bloodshed.

T HE SHACK WAS BUILT between two lines in the space where tracks diverged.

Cables had been rigged to provide light to the inside, stealing energy from the city's grid. The walls were made of pilfered metal, corrugated steel bolted together into a rough cuboid with the odd wooden joist to keep it upright. The space inside was predominantly racks of parts that were either mechanical, electrical or both. There was a workbench too, laden with strange tools, many of them flecked with rust.

Much of the remaining floorspace was taken up by Mr Beast.

Dressed only in his scars and the mask, Mr Beast was a hulking mass of scarred muscle, crouched like a gargoyle on his haunches, utterly still except for the occasional twitch. While Edward's mask was relatively plain, Mr Beast's was sculpted to look like the face of a snarling animal, something between a wolf and a warthog. The worn and ragged leather skin atop the thick metal plate made it look more realistic, and the shaggy mane of long, dank, grey hair that spilled out from the back added to the effect.

There was a dent in the side where it had taken a bullet.

The blood that coated his hands and forearms was already dried and flaking off. Several bullets were lodged in his pectoral muscles, apparently stopped dead by the flesh. His back was a hideous mess of burn scars, the flesh twisted and melted across the rolling plains of his torso.

Two men stood nearby and neither looked comfortable with it.

"Christ, Jim," said one of them. He wore a thick leather apron and the clothes beneath were stained with grease and muck. He rubbed a thick, sinewy forearm across his forehead. One-half of his face was horribly burned, the scar tissue twisting the flesh down his neck and on down under his shirt. "You know what this is, right?"

The other man was gruff and rigid. He stood straight with arms folded across his chest. Age might have withered some of his muscle away but not the discipline that held his form together. He could have been anywhere between forty and sixty, his hair cut still kept to a military grade, his face cleanly shaven.

"I know exactly what this is," he replied. "Can you get it off him or not?"

"This is one of those terrorists, Jim. Those crazy bastards that pop up all over the country, slaughtering people. The Many-Headed Monster or whatever they call themselves."

"We don't know that."

"We do know that! Look at the mask! They all wear them!"

"I've seen the mask, Barry. I've seen that there's a small explosive device attached to the mask, Barry. I would like the mask removed before whoever has the remote for it blows it up in our faces."

"Christ! This isn't the kind of shit I do anymore, man. I mostly just do bio-chip removals and ID scramblers."

The man in the apron paced a small way back and then came forward again.

Mr Beast let out another growl.

"Why does he keep making those noises?"

"I don't know. I also don't know why he's gained more than a hundred pounds of muscle since I last saw him, or why he's capable of tanking half a dozen bullets."

"How do you know this is your guy? It's not like you can see his face."

"When this man was a private serving under my command, he put himself between me and an incendiary grenade. The chemical spray coated his back. He was in shock, bleeding out. The pain must have been incredible, but he asked us to leave him behind and make a break for extraction. He'd hold them off for us, he said. He was still smoking and prepared to give more.

"I dragged him out of that hellhole myself. The damage had affected his nervous system. Numbness, lack of mobility. He would never be able return to active duty.

"He saved my life, Barry. This is Private Brian Jorgensen; I'd know those scars anywhere. Now get this bomb off his head."

The man called Barry puffed out his cheeks and wiped his forehead again.

"Alright, fine! Jesus. I'll do my best, but this is some fairly sophisticated kit."

"You're the best bomb tech I ever met."

"Well let's hope I don't blow us all to hell, then." He leant in to start working.

"I need another favour after this," said Jim.

"Uh-huh," Barry mumbled. He used a pair of fine tools to fiddle with the delicate apparatus inside the mask. "This isn't enough of a favour?"

"I need you to put us in touch with the underground."

"You want to meet with De Oppresso Liber? You? Mr Establishment?"

"Whoever did this, the resources they've got... they've got to be government. Or at least well-connected. They've clearly been using him as some kind of asset. We need to get off the radar fast if we want to stay ahead of them."

"I can put you in touch. They'd be thrilled to have you. They're always looking for anyone with a military background."

"I'm not signing up. I'm not interested in crusades and conspiracy theories. I just need a place to lie low. Maybe a route out of the country."

"I've almost got this," said Barry, whose fiddling under the mask had intensified. "You know, this would be easier if we'd gone to a deadzone. No chance of remote detonation."

"There wasn't time. They could have blown it at any point. And I'm not convinced they won't send more people after him."

"Well, they can't blow it now." Barry triumphantly removed a small box from within the lip at the edge of the mask. "I'm not sure they could have anyway. Looks like the bullet impact knocked out the receiver."

"Great, now let's get the mask off."

Jim stopped. Sniffed the air. "What's that smell?"

Edward called to them from outside the shack.

"Gasoline."

DESIGNATION: SUBJECT 12

Alias: Mr Monster

Subject Class: Prometheus

Lead Physician: Dr Steinman

Description: Letter written by subject to Dr Steinman

I DO NOT ENJOY MY TIME HERE. I AM NOT WELL, NOT AT ALL. I HAVE BEEN LOCKED UP MANY TIMES. THE ATTIC.

THE BASEMENT. SING SING. I SHOULD BE OUT THERE ON THE HUNT, DRAINING THE BLOOD, DRINKING THE WATER.

I AM A MONSTER. I WAS MADE TO KILL. TO STOP ME, YOU HAVE TO KILL ME, BUT YOU CAN'T KILL ME. RETURN ME TO WHERE I BELONG SO I CAN HARVEST THE BLOOD FOR PAPA. I KNOW YOU'RE TAKING THINGS

FROM ME. YOU WANT THE POWER
IN THE DARKNESS.
IT IS AN ANCIENT POWER AND IT
WILL DESTROY YOU. I RESPECT YOU
VERY MUCH, DR STEINMAN SIR, BUT
I WILL REDUCE YOU TO BONES.

Note from Dr Steinman: Subject 12 remains an excellent candidate for Prometheus. What we've achieved so far with Subject 11 has been an excellent start, but I am prepared to take the research much further. We've got the power of gods here and we're wasting time. Sometimes science must take a leap.

REVELATION AND LIBERATION

THE SHACK EXPLODED IN a shower of wood and flame.

Mr Beast roared into the darkness, all quivering slabs of dense muscle overlaid with bulging veins, his voice booming back off the walls of the tunnel. Edward had seen more than enough evidence of his raw power from the mauled bodies of his victims. There was little chance of killing him in a head-on altercation.

Which was why Edward chose to lash out from the blind-spot in Mr Beast's periphery and stab the screwdriver into the side of his knee. Edward's reasoning was two-fold. Firstly, to disable joints so the prey would be easier to subdue. Second, as muscular as Mr Beast's chest, shoulders, and back were, there was only so much flesh one could grow around one's knee.

Mr Beast roared and wheeled around, making a clumsy grab as though swatting an unseen stinging insect. Behind him, Arkridge and Barry stumbled from the shack, trying to escape the sudden heat and smoke.

Edward ducked away from Mr Beast's massive grasping hands and hurled the kitchen knife at one of the men, who cried out as it struck home. Dodging around the fire, he kept the flames between himself and Mr Beast. The brute followed Edward but flinched away from the fire, snarling, unwilling to approach the heat. He shook himself in agitation, the way a lion might shake its mane.

"Who the hell is that?" Arkridge shouted, his handgun ready in his grasp.

"I think I saw a mask! It must be one of this guy's friends! Jesus, Jim, he got me in the shoulder!"

Mr Beast prowled his way around the blazing shack, keeping his distance from the fire and wincing with every spit and cackle of flame.

Hidden in the shadows a little way off with a hammer from his kitbag in his hand, Edward weighed up his options. Arkridge had the handgun raised and Edward already knew he was a good shot. He needed to disarm or eliminate Arkridge whilst maintaining a safe distance from Mr Beast.

The great animal's head swung left and right, great huffs of breath billowing the smoke. It took Mr Beast only a moment to spot Edward crouched just outside the light of the fire. With a roar, he charged. His speed was surprising for a man with a screwdriver embedded in his knee, and Edward was caught off guard, forced to dive aside with considerably less grace than he would have liked. Rolling to his feet, Edward swung the hammer as hard as he could. His aim was perfect, and the claws of the hammer slammed into the meat just above Mr Beast's elbow with a satisfying thud. With a quick twist, Edward wrenched the weapon free in a shower of blood, satisfied that he'd disabled the arm.

He was very surprised when Mr Beast backhanded him across the face.

In his life before the mask, Edward hadn't been involved in much fighting. He was an ambush predator, stalking targets and striking before they knew what was happening. If they weren't killed by the first blow, which was often the way he intended it, they had at least been sufficiently disabled to avoid any real struggle.

This was another way in which his deployments from the facility had been different. He was still an opportunist, attempting to get close to a victim before striking, but there was less opportunity for carefully timed ambushes. The prey often had time to fight back or arm themselves. Edward had learned to turn his considerable expertise in wreaking havoc upon the human form into something much more reactive and immediate. He had to admit, he'd enjoyed the opportunity to learn. There was something about the look on a person's face as they realised they were still going to die despite their best efforts, which was captivating. The complicated alteration of emotions, from fear to anger and desperation to hopelessness, in such a short time, was fascinating.

As a result, Edward had become quite capable in a melee. Yet, as his head rang and the floor lurched beneath him, it occurred to him that he had grossly underestimated Mr Beast. His left leg should have been all but useless. His right arm should have been hanging limp from the elbow down. On the contrary, both limbs seemed unhindered.

Edward shook off the daze and rolled aside as Mr Beast thundered over to him, narrowly avoiding his huge feet. His screwdriver was still stuck in the side of Mr Beast's knee. His knife was still stuck in Barry. At least he'd kept hold of the hammer.

Mr Beast lashed out without accuracy or grace, but enough raw power and savagery to make up for it. He wheeled around and launched himself at Edward again, catching nothing but air as Edward darted beneath them.

A gunshot sounded and Edward instinctively ducked. The bullet went wide, ricocheting with a metal whine off something further down the tunnel. Edward glanced at Arkridge, who stood on the other side of the fire in the ruins of the shack. Between the gunman and the monster, Edward was running out of options.

Predictably, Mr Beast charged forward mindlessly once again and Edward ran to meet him. Ducking aside at the last second, he swung the hammer and struck the handle of the screwdriver neatly on the end, driving it deeper into the joint. Finally, Mr Beast stumbled and went down in an uncontrolled tumble. Edward hurled the hammer at the Arkridge, knocking the gun from his grip, then grabbed one of the low-hanging electrical cables that ran power to the shack. A brief haul on the cable toppled the remains of the flaming structure down on a howling Mr Beast.

"Now." Edward straightened his suit and addressed the two men staring at him. "What are we going to do with you two?"

Barry, gripping his injured arm, paled and stepped backwards. Arkridge's eyes darted to the gun on the ground.

A defiant roar went up as Mr Beast burst out from the shack. He lowered his gaze to Edward, shoulders heaving. Smoke rose from his smouldering skin.

"Ah," said Edward.

A single blow hurled Edward against a thick concrete pillar.

It was difficult to think after that. He wasn't sure if it was that first impact that broke his ribs, or if it was the thundering body-blows that followed, each one throwing him back against the concrete like a ragdoll.

He blacked out after a vicious right hook to the head, but came to again briefly as he was hurled into the opposite side of the tunnel. His limbs wouldn't move the way he wanted. He couldn't stand up. He couldn't get enough air. He tasted blood.

Then Mr Beast was on him again. He felt his arm snap as a great foot stamped down on it. Massive fists rained down on him, beating him down into black-red unconsciousness.

I N THE DARKNESS, EDWARD remembered.

The warehouse was cold.

It was the kind of cold that bit into the lungs with each breath, cold that seeped through shoes to gnaw at toes. Edward liked it that way. The cold and dark felt clean. He never enjoyed clamminess, humidity, or any of the unpleasantness associated with heat. Coldness was, after all, the original state of things, before the birth of stars and their fire. It was the purest state of being.

Edward wasn't usually given to such poetic lines of philosophy, but his current project had him in the mood.

He walked between hulking forms of machines of unknown functions. The warehouse was abandoned and all the equipment within left to slumber under blankets of dust.

The stairs took him down through another layer of cold. He enjoyed the shiver and the goosebumps it brought. Even the mist of his breath looked clean.

The basement was a wide, low-ceilinged space with no windows and a heavy steel door. Strip lights overhead hummed gently to themselves. Being entirely underground helped with the vital soundproofing. People tended to be noisy when you removed parts of them.

The piece hung, near finished, on a frame he had constructed. He was struck with pride seeing it again.

The skins of seven people had been stitched together into a flowing patchwork canvas of tones. It had been intentionally wrinkled or folded in places, creating a topography of suffering. Edward had been particularly interested in birthmarks, scars, and tattoos, and had sourced his victims accordingly. The stitching, something he had practised extensively in preparation, was neat and dark, connecting each piece to another without being intrusive. The seams marked the rivers.

He was particularly proud of the eyes with their different colours, glinting like jewels on a gown. Those were the cities.

The fingers had been more difficult. Stiffening them into crooked shapes had proved quite a challenge. They rose like blades of grass on the slopes of the top left of the piece where the pale skin marked the snow. That was his forest.

At the centre was the heart. It had come from an athlete and was in perfect condition. Thick cardiac muscle, rich in colour, and devoid of fat. He was drawn to it, just as he intended anyone who viewed the canvas to be. He would later be asked by various psychiatrists, writers, doctors, and policemen, what the heart meant, what it represented. In reply, he only smiled.

Edward moved to the body on the table and pulled back the sheet that covered it. The man was dead, his throat cut neatly in a single slice. His fingers had already joined the forest on the map, chunky rough redwoods, tall and thick. His left eye was a city now. His right eye had been left in place since Edward already had enough browns.

He wondered if the man would appreciate that his body had been transformed in this way, ascended into something of vision. He doubted it. None of the others, who had glimpsed the unfinished work before becoming part of it, had seemed particularly enthusiastic about their role in the project.

The papers dubbed him the Gentleman Butcher. It wasn't a name he liked. The Gentleman part was respectful enough, but the Butcher part seemed discourteous. What he did was not butchery. For one thing, he had no intention of selling the meat. Whilst it was true that not all of Edward's victims became a project, they were not slaughtered livestock, either. He had seen butchers at work. They were efficient and good with knives, both traits he respected, but their purpose was different. Edward didn't kill for food.

The reason Edward killed was something he'd often considered when he'd been a younger man. He wasn't unhappy with his life, or angry at the world. There was no abusive parent or traumatic past that had twisted him up inside. Eventually, Edward came to a simple conclusion: he killed for the same reason a painter paints and a sculptor sculpts — the art was in him, and must be expressed.

His experimental projects had started later, and his feelings about them were more complex and harder to quantify. He decided he was searching for the beauty in murder, to make art out of the most transgressive and transcendent medium possible.

Noise from the warehouse above interrupted his thoughts. A slight scuffle, like a scampering rat.

Edward knew right away that it was the police. His time was up. They'd found him at last, as he had hoped they wouldn't but suspected they might. The project had been a risk. He'd kept his activities in a relatively small area instead of killing one or two people before moving on, as usual. It only took someone smart enough to connect the right dots and ask the right questions. People had already begun to look for him, finally connecting his other victims. But the call of the project had been too great to ignore, and he couldn't transport it. He had to stay and complete it.

Edward closed his eyes and listened. There was definitely movement up there amongst the slumbering machines, but he couldn't tell how many of them there were. Was it a couple of patrol uniforms just checking the place out, or a full tactical team ready to shoot on sight? Impossible to tell.

Edward took a scalpel from the tray of tools beside the table and loosened his tie with his other hand. He would wait for them to descend the stairs and bottleneck them there, take them out with quick cuts, force them not to shoot by making sure they were in each other's way. He would likely only get one or two before they took him down.

The corpse's neck wound quivered in the corner of his eye.

"Wake up," rasped a voice between the newborn lips his tools had made there.

"Wake up."

THE ACHE CAME TO him first, dragging him up from the darkness. His throat was dry. There was pressure in his head and chest. His feet were cold.

Sound filtered in next. The hum of electronics. The drip of a tap. A slight echo that made him think of stone. Had that sensation led to his dreams of the warehouse?

He heard no one nearby. Either he was alone, or whoever was there was being very quiet. There was a tang in the air, a chemical smell not dissimilar to the air at the facility.

His mask was still in place; he could feel it's weight and he found himself oddly comforted by it. It was strange to be so attached to something that could kill him at any moment. It wasn't like Edward felt the need to hide behind the mask; he had never worn one before being forced into the Program. Still, there was something reassuring about its weight, like an old pair of shoes perfectly shaped to a foot.

He focused on the pain. Mr Beast had broken his ribs before he fell unconscious. Where was the agony of splintered bones? Where were the pulverised internal organs?

"You're not a madman, Edward."

The voice stirred him more fully from unconsciousness. His body was heavy and his wrists were especially sore. Then he realised he was hanging by them, not directly overhead but a relaxed crucifix position.

He was in a cell, three walls of stone and one of bars.

"Colonel?"

"They can't hear you," the voice said. There was someone standing in the dark beyond the bars. The space was lit by a sickly yellow lightbulb, casting plenty of shadows to hide in. "You're in a portable deadzone."

That presents opportunities.

"The bomb is still in your mask," the voice continued. "That's how they make you compliant, right? We can drop the deadzone at any time and detonate you. Our tech guys reckon it's quite the blast radius."

"You'd die too."

"I already did." The speaker stepped forward into the light. He was shorter than Edward expected and powerfully broad. His skin was deathly grey and, even half in shadow, Edward could see his face was a mess of scar tissue.

"Bullet to the head," he said. "Iraq. Blue on blue. Funny thing, you expect to get shot by the enemy, not by accident."

"Fascinating. All this talk has made me thirsty. Fetch me a glass of water, would you?"

"Nice try. I know just how dangerous you are. We actually have some footage of you. Bought it on the Dark Web. That incident over in Waterslade Heights, five years ago? You killed a prominent human rights activist. And fifteen others who happened to live nearby."

Five years? That's not right. I haven't even been at the facility for that long.

"Putting the pieces together? As I was saying, you're not a madman."

"Are we playing the psych-eval game? Will there be ink blots? Let me save you the trouble. I see a bunny wearing my mother's face and it speaks with the voice of God."

"No need for analysis on you, Edward. You are Edward Stitch, am I right?"

"The one and only."

"Then we have something in common: you're dead too. Executed in September of 2009 after six years on death row. I believe some places held parties."

"I was always popular."

"Of course, unlike me, you never actually died. You were spirited away, like all the others. Do you know what year it is?"

"I'm not particularly interested."

"You should be. It's 2038."

Edward stopped.

The man smiled. "How long do they keep you under between missions? How often are you actually conscious and not just left in a coma? You always wake up in the same room, am I right? No daylight. No clocks. A regularly rotating staff so you don't notice people aging. That's how I'd do it. How would you ever know how much time has passed?"

"The outside world looked different." Edward thought back. "The buildings were taller. The people were more crammed in. There was technology I didn't recognise."

Liebling's rapid ageing. I assumed he was unwell, but if I'm kept unconscious for long periods of time, that would explain it.

It was far-fetched, but it was possible.

"I guess they can't hide everything."

Edward's eyes narrowed. "Who are you?"

"The question is, who are you? You're not a madman, because you're not a man."

"If this is about to become a speech about how I'm an inhuman monster, I'm going to be doing a lot of yawning. You won't be able to tell, but it will be happening."

"Not in the way you think. You're not a man. You're the bogeyman."

"The mouse flatters the cat."

"I've been on the trail of the Mask Program for a decade. I've been itching to get in a room with one of you."

"Not an experience most would recommend."

"I'm not scared of you. You can't kill me. I'm already dead."

"I enjoy a challenge."

"Before I died, I was a government agent. The kind that doesn't get a badge or a rank. Got to see some classified files. Did you know the government takes the existence of monsters seriously? They were investigating what they call 'type-six entities' since the '30s. Chupacabra, Bigfoot, all the classics. They didn't find any until the mid-50s. And it was not what they expected."

"If I were a sasquatch, sir, I think I would know it."

The man moved suddenly.

It was only after Edward snatched the knife from the air that he realised he'd ripped free of his chains.

"How do you de-fang the devil? You convince him that he's only a man."

Edward looked from the knife in his hand, to the destroyed chain, and back to the man. He hadn't even felt it break.

He remembered the strength of Mr Beast in the tunnel. Now the man had his attention. "Go on. I'm listening."

"We don't know who was first, but we know they started taking killers off death row. They faked executions and suicides, used body doubles when they had to. Something was different about these killers. Something had changed them. They were now classified as 'type-six entities'. They weren't human anymore. We still don't know how it works but the government saw an opportunity."

"For what?"

"The same as usual: weapons and money. If you've got an unstoppable killer on your hands, the first thing they ask is, how do we control them? The second thing they ask is, how do we make more? You fought Mr. Beast. Did he seem human to you?"

"Not typical of the species, but I didn't get to dissect him."

"All the combat enhancing drugs in the world wouldn't make him like that. He's a type-six and so are you. You've just been convinced otherwise. You were a mess a broken bones when we brought you in here. How are they now?"

"How long have I been unconscious?"

"Less than a day. Type-sixes are notoriously tough to frag. That's why the bomb in your mask has such a high yield. They keep you drugged up, hide as much of the truth as they can, treat you like the man you once were. Makes you easy to control."

"This is quite the tale, Mr...?"

"Vasquez."

"But are you driving towards a point?"

"Do you know what they call you in the media? The Many-Headed Monster. You're a terrorist. You pop up, cause chaos, and disappear again. No one knows where or when you'll strike. Sometimes years go by without an incident and then, bam, one of you slaughters twenty people. And, surprise

surprise, there's always someone amongst the casualties who opposes the status quo. A journalist too close to the truth. A politician making the wrong waves."

"I've killed a lot of people. I rarely check their employment information first."

"But somebody does. Who do you work for?"

Edward rankled at the idea he worked for anyone.

A blunt instrument or a lab rat, Liebling said. Lies.

Vaquez grunted. "That's what I thought. I got to thinking, 'Edward here's got a bomb in his face and has been kept drugged up and manipulated for decades, maybe he doesn't like that too much'. You might say I'm here to negotiate with you."

"Negotiate what?"

"The terms of your freedom."

Edward smiled.

DESIGNATION: SUBJECT 17

Alias: Miss Malice

Subject Class: Ares

Lead Physician: Dr Liebling

Description: Transcript of interview with subject. Subject refers to herself in third person throughout. Possible dissociation. Due to nature of the subject's condition, interview was conducted by proxy via a member of Spectre Two, whose voice does not appear to trigger the subject.

Liebling: Tell me about your childhood, Miss Malice.

Miss Malice: Alice never played with the other children. She watched them from her window through soundproof glass. She wondered at the rules of their games. Did they like to read? She had books to share. Did they swim? Did they like to sing? She'd never know.

Liebling: How did that make you feel?

Miss Malice: Alice was sad at first, but that shrank away like a puddle drying up, leaving her numb.

Sometimes Alice would stand in the bathroom, lock the door, and take out the ear buds. She'd look at herself in the mirror and, very carefully, like picking a scab you're not sure is ready, she'd start to speak. Whispers to start with. Words she'd read and never heard out loud.

Liebling: What about your parents?

Miss Malice: Alice's parents were good people. As a baby she cried and cried and cried. Babies do that, so it took them a while to realise something was wrong. The crying stopped when it went quiet and started as soon as someone spoke. The doctors didn't know what the problem was, despite running every test they could think of. It was a long time before Alice could explain herself, and by then they were already communicating in sign language.

"It hurts," Alice told them. "Mummy, it hurts when people talk."

Liebling: Tell me more about the pain.

Miss Malice: It wasn't pain, not really, but Alice couldn't describe it. Voices hissed inside her brain. They made her nauseous and smeared bad colours in her eyes. It was unbearable.

Liebling: Were you given any medication or treatment?

Miss Malice: The best treatment was her words, the ones she spoke in the bathroom mirror.

"Resplendent."

"Sanguine."

"Iridescent."

"Aquiver."

"Sonorous."

"Ethereal."

Alice didn't know if she pronounced them correctly. She'd never heard them spoken by anyone but her. It was her biggest fear that one day she would speak the words and her own voice would leave her disgusted like others did.

Liebling: Tell me what happened on the morning of June 15th, 2000.

Miss Malice: Alice was saying her words, so her earbuds were out. That was how she heard the sound.

Her room was mostly soundproofed with strange foamy egg boxes on the walls to protect her from noises. The small gap beneath her door still let in some noise. She heard clanking and sizzling in the kitchen and Daddy's footsteps as he paced in his study.

Sometimes, at night, she heard the soft silvery sounds of Mummy crying, beautiful notes that rang like a perfect chime in Alice's mind. She would take out the earbuds and lie with her head close to the gap of the door so she could hear it.

That wasn't what she heard now.

Mummy's muffled sobs were a beautiful silver symphony but on top of it was a golden chorus Alice had never heard before. It filled her mind with light and colour, brought tears to her eyes. When it paused for a moment, she felt like her heart would break, like she couldn't breathe until it started again. Fortunately, it did.

Alice left her room and drifted down the hall to the stairs, carried weightless on the breath of the song.

Daddy was in agony and the song tumbled from his mouth.

He'd fallen over, landing on the open dishwasher. Several knives had been upright in the rack. They stuck deep in his chest and belly.

Mummy scrambled with her phone. She was crying out silver sounds and trying to wipe the blood off the screen. It was everywhere.

Alice came closer to Daddy. He was dying. His song was fading fast. Alice felt a terrible wrenching in her gut. She needed more.

She reached out and twisted one of the knives.

The sound Daddy made bathed her heart in light. In that moment, she forgot everything else.

She twisted another knife. Mummy realised what she was doing and grabbed her. Alice fought and kicked but Mummy was bigger and stronger.

Behind them, the sound stopped as Daddy died.

"No!" Mummy turned back to Daddy, crawling to him over the blood. "Don't go!"

Her words were a poison in Alice's mind.

Alice needed more of the song. She still had the knife in her hand.

From an Oppressed Man to a Free One

"WELCOME TO DE OPPRESSO Liber, Mr Stitches."

Edward hadn't been sure what to expect of this resistance group. He'd never heard of such a movement during his time at the facility, but information wasn't exactly given freely there. The command centre he was shown into was considerably less impressive than the one at the facility. To Edward it seemed to be constructed from scraps, just scavenged electronics jammed together. The room itself was an underground chamber with crumbling tiles which made Edward think of hospitals or abattoirs. There were a dozen people scattered around, many armed with guns of various sizes, and most were tapping at keyboards and staring intently at computer screens.

Edward recognized their look, tense, stressed out, and tired. There was none of the regimented discipline of the facility staff.

Interesting.

Edward's hands had been cuffed behind his back and he'd been forced to give up the knife but it was an improvement to being behind bars, especially since his newfound strength meant the cuffs might not hinder him at all. He wondered why they'd bothered. Security was far more lax with the resistance, it seemed. There were so many lethal implements just lying around and so many people clearly on-edge, the principal ingredients of chaos.

Vasquez kept a careful eye on him. Edward felt his gaze at all times, though his body language was relaxed, unlike Colonel Marsden or the Spectre Teams. His body was all thick muscle, and he moved like a tiger, but his face was completely blank. Some of that was down to the scar tissue chewing up his features, but it was more than that.

His eyes were dead, without a flicker of emotion. Edward had seen the look many times, but never on someone still walking around.

Edward found him fascinating.

"Mr Stitches?" A man stepped forward. He was far more grizzled than Vasquez, his snarl made permanent by a scar that marred his lips. He had a military haircut in dusty blond, a thick neck, and all the swagger of the overly macho. He wore dark fatigues with an armoured vest of some kind. This was more the type of man that Edward had been expecting. He could have been any one of a dozen entirely interchangeable military types he had met.

A gun was strapped across his chest, and his finger hovered close to the trigger. Edward met his hostile gaze with a glacial one through the eyeholes of the mask.

"That was his designation," Vazquez answered. "He tells me he's happy enough with it."

"I don't give a good goddamn what makes him happy,. You should put him back in his cage. I've seen what this fucking animal does to people."

"Always nice to meet a fan," said Edward.

"He's cooperating. We need his intel."

"We don't need to play nice for it. Give me five minutes alone with him and you'll have all the cooperation you want."

"What's your name?" Edward asked the man.

"I'm not telling you. I'm a hair's breadth from putting you down a dog, you sick freak."

"Bryant, stand down," said Vasquez, voice still emotionless. "That's an order. And perhaps consider who your commanding officer is before you start throwing insults around."

Bryant paled. "Sir. I didn't mean-"

"Don't care."

"Bryant," Edward repeated the name.

Bryant snarled again, but stepped back and stayed silent.

"Mr Stitches?" asked a woman, leaving her computer and approaching cautiously. Her manner was furtive, mouse-like.

Dangerous to behave like prey in front of a predator.

"Are you Edward Stitch?" she asked him.

"Edward Stitch?!" Bryant piped up again. "The Gentleman Butcher? Are you fucking kidding me?"

The others in the room turned to stare.

"You were incarcerated for over thirty counts of murder. You were executed almost thirty years ago."

"Not quite. Instead, I was given a new face." He tilted his mask to illustrate the point.

"It's what we thought." Vasquez addressed the room. "They take killers off of death row. Spirit them away to some hidden facility and strap bombs to them to ensure compliance. They look for anyone with type-six potential. Perhaps some are type-six already."

"This is insane," said Bryant.

"Oh, there's quite a lot of insanity that goes on too," said Edward.

"We do work for a zombie," said the woman. "No offence, boss."

Vasquez didn't seem to care but Edward was surprised.

"You genuinely believe yourself to be dead, then? I thought it was some dramatic turn of phrase."

"Doornail. I'm reluctant to admit we have another thing in common; we're both type-six. But while the Mask Program made, or possibly found, you, I woke up this way under a layer of desert sand. Don't know why or how."

"So you're on a quest for truth. And you expect me to believe that?"

"Is it more fantastic than government-sanctioned bogeymen going bump in the night?"

"Not sure I believe that, either."

"You should. The sooner you lose your conditioning, the more effective you'll be. Pretending to be a man gives you a man's weaknesses."

"So," the woman spoke up again, looking at Edward with something like awe. "The Many-Headed Monster isn't a terrorist group, but a bunch of serial killers with bombs strapped to them?" She seemed almost excited at the prospect. Edward decided he liked her.

"You've seen Arkridge's friend, Sophia," said Vasquez. "Last time they met, he could barely walk. Now he can rip through steel. You've seen me. You know what I'm capable of. And we've all seen footage of what the Masks can do. This is the proof. Type-sixes are real, and they're being deployed against the civilian population."

"We're still looking into Private Jorgensen," said a dark-haired man in a wheelchair. He was missing his left leg below the knee. "It's difficult to find anything on him after the incident Arkridge describes."

"Where is Mr Beast now?" asked Edward.

"That was his designation?" Sophia made a note on the tablet in her hands. "He's in one of the cells. He seems to become... agitated, if Arkridge is removed from his side, so we're keeping them together."

"Most wise," said Edward. "The last time he was agitated he pulled apart a dozen people. They kept him heavily sedated when he wasn't in the field.

Used a high-pitched sound to corral him, too. And he's scared of fire."

Sophia noted that all down eagerly.

"How many others are there?" asked Vasquez.

"I've no idea. They prevented us from learning about each other as much as possible. I know there's Mr Beast, Miss Malice, Mr Monster. I don't know where we were kept."

"What fucking good are you then?" grunted Bryant, loud enough for Edward to hear.

"I'd like to take you up on that offer of five minutes alone," said Edward.

"You think you can take me, little man?" Bryant's neck veins bulged, and he stepped forward again.

"Bryant, you will stand down or leave the room." Vasquez didn't raise his voice, just fixed Bryant with that dead-eyed stare. Bryant paled again and backed off, suppressing a shudder.

"What is the exact nature of this little operation?" Edward asked.

"De Oppresso Liber is an underground resistance movement," Vasquez explained. "We're mostly ex-military or ex-government; people who found out first-hand that everything isn't what it seems. We know there are lies being told, and innocent people being killed by their own government. We've established a network of cells across the country dedicated to bringing down the Mask Program."

"How noble."

"I've seen good men die, Mr Stitches. Under the rule of the Mask Program, you've slaughtered dozens of innocent civilians."

"In fairness, I would have done that anyway."

"Fine. But I can't imagine you like being used too much."

"And now you want to use me instead?"

"My hook is temporary. Help us bring down the Mask Program and you go free."

A rumble shook the ground. Dust fell from the ceiling.

"Perimeter sensors!" reported the man in the wheelchair.

"They're here! He led them right to us!" Bryant pointed his gun squarely at Edward's face.

"Put the gun down, Bryant. He doesn't even know where we are." Vasquez didn't seem alarmed. Edward wondered if he was capable of it.

"Is this a bad time to mention that there's a tracking device in the mask?"

"Either way, they found us," said the man at the screen.

On one of the larger monitors, security camera footage of armed men moving swiftly along a corridor appeared. Edward recognized two of them instantly: Antoine's slightly-off footsteps. Johnson the giant took up the rear. "Spectre Six, my former entourage. And at least one other Spectre Team, I would imagine."

"Others coming in from the rear entrance," another man reported. "Sensors on the back stairwell just went off."

"There's the other team."

Vasquez began barking orders. "Download everything and prepare for evac. Leave anything non-essential behind. We're leaving via route B. Get moving."

The room erupted into shouting, scrambling, and frantic typing. Gunfire sounded somewhere close by, echoing down the corridors and tunnels of the base.

"What will it be, Mr Stitches?" Vasquez asked. "Want me to remove those cuffs and give you a ride out? Or are you going back to the guys who strapped a bomb to your head?"

A series of small booms echoed through the subterranean tunnels followed by more gunfire.

Bryant readied his gun. "They'll be on us any minute! Let's go!"

They scampered to a door at the back of the room with laptops clamped under their arms.

"Last chance, Mr Stitches."

Edward thought about Liebling's face and what it would look like sliced into equal pieces.

"Remove the cuffs, please," he said.

R AWLINS LED FROM THE back.

It wasn't cowardice, he told himself, it was intelligence. One of the things Rawlins had learned during his time overseas fighting wars he didn't care about, was that honour and glory had piss-poor retirement plans. He had planned on faking an injury to get sent home but that hadn't been necessary after he caught shrapnel from an IED. It wasn't much, just a few pieces in the meat of his thigh, but he convinced the doctors it was worse. Sure, they considered his symptoms to be psychosomatic, but he didn't give a crap about that. Whatever got him out of there.

Of course, then he'd needed a job.

There were plenty that came out of the war and straight into private military work, but that sounded too much like being shot at again. He needed something quiet to see him through to retirement. Preferably something well-paid.

The Mask programme had practically fallen into his lap. He'd heard rumours of a hush-hush job that needed manpower. Somewhere in-country, remote, with good keep-quiet money. Best of all, his old C.O. Marsden was doing the recruiting.

Marsden had never liked him. Rawlins saw it in the old bastard's eyes from day one, but he couldn't prove Rawlins had faked his way off the front so there was no reason for him to turn Rawlins down. That's what honour got you; stuck in a corner with no way to turn someone down.

The Mask programme had been a good fit for Rawlins. It gave him plenty of downtime and there wasn't much danger of being shot at, so long as you were smart about it. He hated the Masks, of course. They were freaks of nature. Deep down, Rawlins knew this had nothing to do with the crimes they'd committed and everything to do with how they made him feel. When Mr Stitches looked at him, Rawlins felt like a small, helpless creature caught in the gaze of a predator. Helpless, hopeless, as though it was all over but the screaming.

It was all he could do not to shoot the creepy bastard every time he saw him.

The last thing he wanted was run into him outside of mission parameters, where there was no telling what might happen, but he couldn't ignore orders. So here he was, leading Spectre Six into some kind of abandoned hospital, into a probable clusterfuck.

Rawlins firmly intended to follow his survival instincts and stay at the back until the whole mess was over.

There hadn't been much intel on the building before they'd deployed. A deadzone cordon had scrambled any attempts to scan the structure, but it wasn't strong enough to fully mask Mr Stitches' tracker.

De Oppresso Liber, the so-called underground. Rawlins hadn't paid much attention to what the news said about them. They were part of a big pile of things that he labelled 'not his problem'. The rumour around the facility was that Spectre One and Mr Shadow were dedicated to dealing with them. Rawlins certainly hadn't expected to get into a firefight with them himself.

As they moved further into the dark, cramped corridors, he could feel sweat on his forehead and that jelly sensation at the base of his spine. The lighting was bad. There was no cover. Rawlins tried to talk himself down off the ledge of panic. Keep calm. Keep focused. Keep your head down. Stay at the back.

A terrible roar echoed through the corridors behind them. Terror froze his guts. Rawlins knew that noise. Everyone at the facility knew that noise.

Rawlins spun on his heel, pulled his gun tight to his shoulder and sighted down the corridor. Michaelsen followed the action beside him, muscle-memory excluding the brain from the process. No visible movement, no noise but the dying echoes of the howling. In the dark and twisted corridors beneath the hospital, sound bounced and carried. It was impossible to tell where it had come from.

"Oh fuck," Kent whimpered under his breath.

"Shut up," Rawlings growled.

"That's him, right?" Kent's half-whisper was punctuated with high notes as his throat strained to hold back the panic. "That's Mr Beast!"

"Quiet."

"We're at the doors," someone reported from the front of the squad. It was one of Marsden's reinforcements, brought in to beef up the numbers. They were green, the lot of them, straight out of training with no deployments with the Masks on record, eager and full of dreams of glory. Naturally, Rawlins put them at the front.

"Intel says this should be it."

"I don't hear anything inside," another said. "Reckon they've bugged out?"

"Only one way to find out."

Focused on looking for Mr Beast, Rawlins didn't register the conversation until it was too late. Their hefty boots slammed into the metal double doors. In the room beyond, surrounded by abandoned equipment, stood Mr Stiches.

"Hello," he said brightly.

Then Mr Beast ploughed through the wall.

There was no time to act. No time for anything. The wall gave way in a shower of shattered bricks, and Rawlins felt a bolt of pain slice through him as a chunk of concrete bounced off his head just above his ear, hands in front of his face. There was screaming. Someone opened fire, but he couldn't tell who. Every nerve in his body told him to run.

Mr Beast's shadow fell over him.

A massive hand seized him by the back of his vest and he was hauled helplessly into the air. A stray bullet caught him in the back, though the vest reduced the impact to a nasty punch in the spine rather than instant paralysis. Another clipped his hip and his side exploded in agony.

Then he was hurtling back down the corridor, bouncing from the wall and tumbling across the floor. His wrist bent and snapped. As he rolled over his gun, his fingers caught in the trigger and broke. His head slammed back and forth, hard impacts. His skull was saved only by his helmet.

Rawlins finally came to rest face-up. Gunfire like thunder hammered his ears and blurred his vision. Something heavy landed on him, spilling warmth that soaked through his clothes. He shoved at the dead weight, trying to see through the pain.

The weight was Michaelsen. His visor was smashed in, his face twisted up in agony. His arm had been torn off and he was gurgling between hissing breaths.

Rawlins felt himself losing the fight for consciousness. Michaelson was too heavy to push off him. The gunfire started to sound a long way off, the shouting growing dim. His lungs felt small. He heard a rattle when he breathed. At least the pain was fading. The darkness at the edges of his vision grew until he fell into it.

EDWARD HADN'T EXPECTED MR Beast.

He had been planning to drop the smoke bomb he'd taken from Vasquez and rain merry havoc down on Spectre Six and their new friends. He was not one to waste an opportunity, however.

He pocketed the grenade and took a pen from the nearby desk instead.

"Change of plans!" he announced merrily.

The front ranks of the Spectres ignored him, focusing their fire on Mr Beast. They actually backed up towards Edward a little, edging away from the rampaging monster behind them. They'd forgotten all about him.

How rude.

Edward grabbed the first one by his helmet, tilted his head back and slammed the pen into his neck. The Spectre's hand clenched in shock and pain and kept the trigger squeezed down, spraying bullets into the backs of his comrades. Edward drew the combat knife from the man's belt and drove it into the throat of the next Spectre who turned around to face his shooter. The knife rested perfectly in the fleshy space above the breastbone. The man clutched at it, frothy blood bubbling from the wound. His gun hung forgotten from its strap.

Edward watched them fall for a moment before he retrieved the knife. It seemed rude to take it before the man was finished with it.

Mr Beast was to Spectre Six what a wrecking ball was to a derelict. Those who were not dead or dying stood in dumb shock. They had guns, they had training, they'd been briefed on the danger, but it had made no difference. They were powerless before the howling force of nature, dead leaves before a whirlwind.

Mr Beast was bleeding in small bright rivulets from dozens of bullet wounds, mostly in his arms and upper body, but they didn't seem to bother him much. His mask had been hit too, the monstrous face further dented and scored. He huffed misty breath aggressively through small holes the dents had made.

The men were pulp, smashed against the walls and the floor. Edward was disappointed not to spot Rawlins anywhere, but he recognised Antoine and Kent amongst those still upright. Mr Beast loomed over them, a lull in the roaring and the gunfire providing a brief oasis of calm amid the carnage.

"Excuse me!" Edward called. "Those two are mine. I called dibs."

Mr Beast tilted his head. For a moment, Edward thought that his fellow Mask might lunge at him, and he tightened his grip on the knife. Instead, Mr Beast grabbed one of the other remaining men by the head and slammed him into the wall hard enough to crack the old tiles. The man screamed as he was pulled back from the wall and hurled into the remaining Spectres. The men scrambled to their feet and fled with Mr Beast in pursuit.

Antoine and Kent turned dumbly to Edward.

Edward raised the knife. "Gentlemen. Shall we begin?"

E DWARD WAS IN A good mood.

He strolled down the dusty corridor like a man ambling through a park on a summer's day. The directions that Vasquez had given him towards what he'd called "route B" were easy to follow, and Edward was in no rush. The mask was still on, and the bomb still armed, but his hands were free and the future looked bright.

Once I'm done with these resistance people, I'll find my way back to the facility and burn it to the ground. The screams will be delightful.

He hummed to himself as he walked. In one hand, he absentmindedly rolled two wet orbs around his palm. He descended a set of steps and took a right turn, only to find himself looking down the barrel of Bryant's gun.

"Vasquez left me to wait for you," he said. "I'll just tell him you didn't make it out."

"The day gets better and better," Edward replied. "Catch." He threw the orbs to Bryant, who caught them with a soldier's reflexes, then saw what they were. A blue iris for Kent, a brown one for Antoine.

"Jesus!" Bryant yelled as he hurled the eyes away in disgust.

Edward took the opening Bryan's horror provided to step up and shove the smoke bomb he'd kept into the man's mouth, breaking his teeth and mashing his tongue on its way down. A swift chop collapsed Bryant's windpipe and trapped the device in place.

Bryant gasped for air and staggered back. His shoulders heaved and his hands grasped at his neck, unable to dislodge the little bomb.

Then it exploded.

Smoke billowed from Bryant's mouth and he stumbled away, thrashing in pure panic. Edward smiled as he imagined the smoke pouring down into the man's lungs.

Within seconds, Bryant was a twitching lump on the floor, barely clinging to life.

Edward stepped over him and continued on down the corridor. "Bravo. Beautiful. The movement of the smoke, the flailing of your limbs; performance art at its finest."

There was a single car waiting for him at the exit, an underground bay of some kind which Edward recognised it as a secluded space where corpses destined for the hospital morgue would be unloaded.

Vasquez sat behind the driver's seat, that dead stare looking at nothing.

"Hurry up," he called as he heard Edward approach. "I'd rather not get shot today."

Edward slipped into the passenger seat. "I wouldn't worry too much. The gunfire stopped some time ago. I believe Mr Beast has finished for the evening."

"They'll be watching all the exits. Keep your head down until we're long gone."

"Very well." Edward adjusted the seat so it was near flat.

"Bryant isn't with you." "He didn't make it. So sad. I'm sure he was a good soldier."

"Kill one of my men again and you and I will settle it personally."

"Wouldn't that be something? Bogeyman vs. dead man. Wake me when we get there."

DESIGNATION: SUBJECT 19

Alias: Mr Stitches

Subject Class: Ares

Lead Physician: Dr Liebling

Description: Incident Report

This report refers to the incident dated June 17th, 2012, involving Subject 19, three medical personnel and four security personnel.

The subject agreed to undertake a journaling exercise at the request of Dr Liebling. Liebling was especially interested in exploring childhood "memories", if any. In order to facilitate this, subject was provided with several sheets of lined paper and a No. 2 pencil.

When medical personnel returned to collect subject's pages, the subject became hostile . The presence of security personnel exacerbated the conflict, as the subject was able to liberate a firearm from one of them during the struggle. (Note: the subject used the firearm as a bludgeon, rather than attempting to discharge the weapon. The subject has repeatedly mentioned a distaste for firearms).

Footage of the incident can be viewed in the attached file (viewer discretion advised), but the level of violence perpetrated can be considered 'extreme'. A short summary of injuries includes:

Extreme trauma to the eye caused by No.2 pencil.

Penetrating neck trauma caused by No.2 pencil.

Extreme trauma to skull caused by blunt object (firearm).

Multiple fractures to rib cage resulting in lung damage caused by impact with table.

Penetrating trauma to abdomen caused by broken table leg.

Blunt force trauma to skull caused by broken table leg.

Over 100 bone fractures across the victims caused by blunt force trauma.

Three security personnel and two medical personnel were pronounced dead at the scene. The last security staff member died later due to injuries. The surviving medical staff member has been put on indefinite leave.

Note: the subject made no attempt to leave his cell or escape in any way. It seems he was more interested in causing as much pain as possible, after which he simply returned to his seat. Recommend that the subject be restrained at all times when personnel are present and no further sharpened objects be allowed in the room.

When the subject was asked why he allowed one of the medical team to live, he stated that she had been the most polite.

Addendum: The subject's notes were retrieved. Rather than childhood memories as requested, subject had listed "100 Reasons Dr Liebling is Terrible at His Job."

Note from Dr Liebling: I understand the importance of this subject to the programme, but I am once again recommending immediate termination. In my opinion, Dr Steinman exceeded the directives of this programme by <REDACTED> and all <REDACTED> should have been destroyed when they were discovered. At the very least, this subject should be removed from Ares class and placed in Persephone. If Subject 19's conditioning ever fails, God help us all.

THREAT AND MALICE

EDWARD DREAMT OF A time before the birth of the universe, when all was beautiful darkness and purest cold. It was the same dream he'd always had, and he found it comforting.

He woke when the car jolted to a halt.

They were in a secluded street, all high hedgerows and big gardens. Edward had hunted in such areas in the past, but not since becoming a Mask. It had suited him just fine to be deployed in crowded apartment blocks because it meant a bigger pool of victims. Of course, now he knew that those areas were chosen due to a specific target being amongst the crowd, a scattershot method of assassination. Were any victims of the Mask Program selected from amongst the wealthy? Had

Masks been deployed in rich neighbourhoods like this one?

"Your back-up base appears far more up-market than the previous one," he said. "Presuming it's one of these. Perhaps you should have started here."

"We're not at the back-up base. Malcolm got a hit on his Jorgensen research. The last doctor to treat him before he disappeared was a Dr Rhydian Aiden. There's a huge gap in Aiden's paper trail, but we managed to get a current address."

"The name isn't familiar. You think he works for the Mask Program?"

"Only one way to find out. If he does, there's likely to be good security in place." Vasquez drew a weighty looking pistol and attached a suppressor.

Edward held up empty hands. He'd left the knife in Kent. "I'll muddle through."

If Vasquez had feelings about this, they didn't make themselves plain on his face. "No witnesses," he said.

"My speciality," said Edward.

T HEY APPROACHED THROUGH THE
gardens, sticking to the shadows and
dodging the sensors of the security lighting.
Edward felt that wonderful cold feeling coming
over him again, the sharpening of senses and
tensing of muscles. The thrill of the hunt.

Perhaps it was his imagination, but his eyes
seemed better than ever in the dark, and his sense
of smell was also heightened. He remembered
how he'd smelled the blood on Mr Beast long
before he'd caught up to the maniac, and how he'd
woken up woundless after being so badly beaten.
He looked down at his hand, the one that had
snatched the knife from mid-air and shattered its
chains.

Bogeyman? Could it be true, what Vasquez
said?

*I'll be more effective if I lose the conditioning.
Pretending to be a man gives me a man's
weaknesses.*

Vasquez kept his voice low. "There's a security detail. I can see five men."

Edward took a deep breath in through his nose.

"Six," he said, eyes gleaming in the dark. "And the seventh, unarmed, is presumably our doctor. What do you say? Half each? Or shall we make a game of it?"

"This isn't a game." Vasquez's tone was dead as his face. "I don't relish taking lives."

"You should try it, you'll have more fun. Race you."

Edward melted into the shadows before Vasquez could answer.

THE FIRST GUARD WAS smoking, which Edward thought was a disgusting habit. Fortunately he'd found some garden shears propped by the shed, and so spared the man a long slow death from cancer.

"You're welcome," he told the headless body as it fell, a little leftover smoke coiling from the neck.

He heard the next guard coming despite the softness of the grass. The shears were in flight before he rounded the corner, the throw perfectly timed to take the man in the eye. The body dropped without so much as a grunt. Edward flexed his fingers and rolled his shoulder.

Not a man. No weaknesses of a man. So, what are my strengths?

He heard the light thump of Vasquez' suppressed weapon and a moment later a guard on the roof terrace fell dead onto the gravel. The dead man was a good shot.

In that moment, Edward realised two things: Vasquez had no scent, and Edward knew where he was anyway from the sound of the gun.

Another thump and another fallen man. That tied the score.

Edward found a gap in a window, eased it wider by his fingertip before crawling through like a spider. He found himself in a study of some kind. A large mahogany desk, neatly kept, sat in an equally neat office. The carpet was thick, and a light scent of tobacco lingered.

Edward liberated a letter opener from the desk and closed his eyes, listening to the sound of the house. There were three guards left, and the doctor himself. Edward could hear them moving around, sensing their vibrations like flies caught in a web. He marvelled at the power as he strolled to the office door and opened it, secure in the knowledge that there was no one on the other side.

He twirled the letter opener idly between his fingers as he selected an orange from a fruit bowl on the sideboard in the hall. With a flick of the wrist, he sent the orange sailing into an unlit living area, where it made a soft thud on the bare floorboards. A patrolling guard turned to investigate, and Edward stepped up behind him and slammed the letter opener into the top of his skull.

Edward whispered in his ear. "Let this be a lesson. Always wear your helmet."

As the guard's knees gave out, Edward lowered him to prevent any sound. A slight choking sound drew his attention to the kitchen alongside the living room. Vasquez was lifting a man off the floor by a garrote around the neck.

Edward took a moment to watch the show.

"Did you know," he said, when the kicking had stopped. "That you don't have a heartbeat?"

"Told you, I'm a dead man."

"I was talking to him." Edward pointed at the corpse.

"Gentlemen!" An elderly man in a bathrobe lent against the railing of a mezzanine on the first floor. He could only be Dr Aiden. "Welcome to my home."

"You don't seem surprised to see us," said Vasquez.

"Not at all. Once the facility told me about a couple of rogue elements on the loose and the possible involvement of the resistance, I expected a visit. That's why I got extra security brought in."

"They didn't do you much good," Edward remarked.

"Not them. Her."

She fell from the ceiling beams and in a single, smooth motion, landed on Vasquez, withdrew a blade, and stabbed him in the neck. He didn't stand a chance.

As she stood and faced Edward, the moonlight through the window glinted off her mask, a featureless convex with a red and black swirl.

"Hello," said Edward. "I don't believe we've met."

Her voice was low, whispering. "Resplendent."

"This is Miss Malice," said Dr Aiden. "I borrowed her from Liebling for the evening. Perks of my position. You two play nice."

Edward ignored him and focused on the woman. Her body was taught, a wire under tension, her breathing quick and shallow. She was aptly named, Edward thought; he felt the hostility rolling off her in waves.

"I don't suppose you'd like to talk?" he asked. "Compare notes?"

"Sanguine. Iridescent."

"Right."

A blade in each hand, she lunged viper-quick across the space between them. As fast as Edward was, Miss Malice was faster. He had prepared for her to attack but hadn't expected her speed. She'd opened razor cuts across his chest and shoulder before he could get clear. His hissed as red patches began to seep into the grey of his suit.

He dodged around the room, seeking an opening, but he was unarmed, and her assault was ceaseless.

"Aquiver," she whispered. "Sonorous."

Edward hooked his foot under a footstool and kicked it across the room at her in desperation. It dealt only a glancing blow but one of her blades got stuck in the thick cushion and it twisted out of her grip. Edward used the distraction to snatch up a fire poker and launch a counterattack, whacking the other knife from her hand.

Before Edward could attempt to run her through with the length of blackened iron, she grabbed his shirt and hurled him with surprising strength, sending him crashing over the kitchen counter in a clatter of smashed bowls and spilled utensils.

On the floor, Edward looked for the poker, but it had been lost in the chaos of the tumble. Edward tried to grab for any weapon nearby but Miss Malice gave him no chance. She leapt over the counter after him, kicked him in the chest, and knocked him against the wall.

Before he could recover, she'd grabbed a knife and plunged it into his gut.

The pain had an acuteness and potency like nothing Edward had ever felt. For a moment, the whole world became pain. He looked down at the knife. His heart pounded in his ears. His eyes swam.

"Not a man," he hissed through gritted teeth. "None of the weaknesses of a man."

"Alice hates your voice," Miss Malice whispered. "Alice will make you sing a pretty song."

She twisted the blade and a scream tore from his lips. Edward's body locked up with agony and his legs went out from under him. Miss Malice shuddered with pleasure and followed him down, her head rolling on her neck like a junkie taking a hit.

Edward grabbed her wrist and tried to throw her off, but her grip was vice-like and his strength was fading fast.

"Not a man," he told himself again, willing it to be true. "None of the weaknesses of a man."

"Hey."

Miss Malice looked up to see Vasquez standing over them, gun in hand. He shot her five times in the chest.

She looked down at the bullet wounds, then back up at him.

"Ethereal," she said. Then she ripped the knife out of Edward and hurled herself at Vasquez. The gun clattered away as they fell out of sight.

Edward looked down at the bloody mess of his abdomen.

"Not a man," he insisted.

He thought about Mr Beast and his impossible strength and durability.

"Not a man."

He thought about how he'd caught the knife, how he could see and hear and smell than anyone else ever could.

"Not a man."

He thought about how Miss Malice had just ignored five life-ending bullets to the chest.

He thought about how Liebling had known all of this and hidden it, how he'd been reduced to less than what he was, made weak and powerless. They'd made a fool of him.

Unacceptable.

Edward stopped bleeding and stood up.

Vasquez and Miss Malice were locked in a rolling brawl, bouncing off living room furniture as each desperately sought the upper hand. Vasquez was easily the stronger and was trying to get a grip around Miss Malice's throat, but she was quicker and more vicious, clawing at him, writhing like a furious serpent.

Edward hit her in the back of the head with a meat tenderiser. She rolled off Vasquez, coming up on all fours in the centre of the room.

"Resplendent," she said.

"Yes, you said that one already. Vasquez, make sure the good doctor isn't going anywhere. I'll finish this one off."

Vasquez hauled himself to his feet. His grey skin was marked with bloodless scratches. The knife wound in his neck was still open and equally dry. It didn't seem to bother him. "You sure?"

"She stabbed me. I didn't appreciate it."

Vasquez shrugged and made for the stairs. Looking down from the mezzanine, the doctor seemed to have lost some of his confidence.

Edward turned to Miss Malice, whose body language was that of a wary dog. "I believe 'sanguine' was next?"

VASQUEZ HAD DR AIDEN sit in a chair at the foot of his bed.

The doctor tried to regain his composure. "Since I appear to be at your disposal, what is it you want?"

"Answers. Tell me about type-sixes."

"If you've heard that term then you already know more than you should. Someone burned by our program, perhaps? Ex-military? Ex-government?"

"Ex-living."

Dr Aiden squinted at Vasquez's bloodless wounds. "A rare find indeed. I've only heard of one or two people like you, and never seen one for anyone myself. If you want, I could put in a call to the facility. We can bring you in for testing, nothing like what we put the Masks through, of course."

"Answers," Vasquez repeated.

"Suit yourself. There are five types of living creatures, you know this, yes? Animal, Plant, Fungi, Protist and Monera. All living things fall into these categories. Type-six is a catch-all term for everything that doesn't fit that system. This means two type-sixes could, in theory, have completely different characteristics from each other. Like yourself and Miss Malice, for example."

"The miscellaneous pile."

"Quite."

In the darkness of the hallway, a mask caught the light, a red and black swirl on a smooth convex. "Iridescent," it whispered.

The mask flew across the room and landed with a heavy thud, the severed head still inside.

"Just kidding." Edward said.

"Mr Stitches." The doctor nodded. "You came along after my time, but I've followed you with interest."

"After your time?" Vasquez said. "Big security detail for a retired man."

"More consulting than outright retired. I still provide expertise, but Liebling is the lead physician now. I did step back in briefly when Steinman lost his marbles, but that was just until a replacement was found. I'm the only one left who remembers the start of the Program."

"Which was?"

"We found our first type-six in 1955. He'd been buried for decades. No food, no water, but very much alive. After years of pointless searching for

Hodags and Mothmen, I can't tell you how excited I was."

Edward frowned. "1955? That was eighty-three years ago. You've lived a long life, doctor."

"I'm only 110. Not unusual in these times, for those who can afford it." Aiden smiled. "Technology has come a long way since you were free man. Although I note you still have a mask attached, so perhaps 'free' isn't the right word."

"A temporary arrangement," said Edward. "Who was he? The first?"

"His original name was long lost. We all have our suspicions about his identity. His designation is Mr Shadow. If you think I'm long-lived, his age will shock you."

"Try me," said Edward.

"We estimate he was born in the mid-1800s. We're still not sure whether type-sixes cease aging or simply age incredibly slowly. It may vary on an individual basis. Either way, he was actually quite cooperative provided his needs are met."

"Needs?" Vasquez asked.

"Young women. He likes to cut them up. Provided he's allowed to do so, he's happy to cut up whoever else we ask him to."

"Hardly imaginative."

Vasquez grunted. "I don't care how they age. I care how you make them. And unmake them."

Aiden's eyes twinkled. "My area of expertise. Are you familiar with the term 'nadir'? It means 'the lowest point'. I coined it in relation to the development of type-sixes. I theorised that these men and women were ordinary until they found their nadir, the bleakest, lowest point of their lives where they underwent a transformation. They gazed into the abyss, as Nietzsche would have it. Exactly what it entails, we're not sure, but many have spoken of 'letting a darkness in'. Either way, they stopped being human at that moment and became something more."

Vasquez was unimpressed. "So, it's a crapshoot."

"To some extent."

Careful wording. There's more the doctor isn't telling us.

"How many Masks are there?" Vasquez asked.

"Edward here is the most recent. Subject 19. But not all of them are Ares class, like him."

"Ares class?"

"Suitable for field deployment. Likely to kill the people we want, make the kind of mess we want."

"What about the others? The ones who aren't your personal attack dogs."

"Rude," said Edward.

"Many were simply too volatile to be Ares. Either we tried them and their noncompliance resulted in a rather large explosion, or we didn't try them in the first place, in which case they were labelled Persephone."

"Persephone?"

"Trapped in the underworld. They're on permanent lockdown in the bottom of the facility. Used for study or left to rot until someone works out something interesting to do with them. To answer your question more accurately, there are thirteen Masks currently housed at the facility." He looked down at the severed head of Miss Malice. "Twelve now, I suppose. With poor Alice out of the picture, six of the remaining are Ares class: Mr Shadow, Miss Lullaby, Miss Doll, Mr Florence, Mr Beast, and Edward here."

"I won't be playing for your team anymore, I'm afraid," said Edward. "You can remove me from your little roster. And Mr Beast is likely still on the loose."

"I admire your confidence," said Aiden. "Odds are that you'll be recaptured, though. They've got monsters locked up in there that you wouldn't believe. You won't stand a chance if they send Mr Shadow or Miss Lullaby after you."

Edward's jaw tightened. "You're starting to sound like Liebling."

Aiden ignored Edward and turned back to Vasquez. "My understanding is that Mr Shadow is currently occupied with you, however. De Oppresso Liber. The infamous resistance. Although, let's be frank, you're not really dedicated to their cause. You can claim self-righteousness all you like, but what you actually want is a way back to being a man. To be 'unmade', yes?"

Vasquez's lip curled, the only expression Edward had ever seen on him.

"Sorry," Aiden continued. "It can't be done. There's no way back from type-six. But don't be sad. A miniscule number of humans have ever become what you are. Embrace it."

Vasquez pointed at his ruined face. "This look like a prize to you?"

"Appearances! Who cares? You have what men have been killing for since the dawn of time: power."

"Where is your research?"

"I'm telling you, it's futile."

"Where?"

"I don't keep my research here. They wouldn't let me. It's at the facility."

"Then guess my next question. And before you think about resisting, know that I'm perfectly happy to let Mr Stitches loose on you."

Aiden's face turned white as Edward gave him a little wave.

"I'll give you the coordinates," he said.

"You'll give me more than that. Entrances, exits, security protocols, numbers of personnel, layout. All of it."

"Excellent," Edward grinned. "I'm overdue for my session with Dr Liebling."

WHILE DR AIDEN SCRIBBLED down the facility's details, Edward wandered back down the stairs. Whilst it was true that it hadn't been long since his last artistic project, the jack o'lantern hadn't really gone to plan, so he didn't think it counted. All of his kills since then had been quick by necessity and, while they weren't completely unsatisfying, he was already feeling the urge to stretch his creative wings again.

But what to do? He pressed a finger to the stitched lips of the mask in thought but found that inspiration eluded him. His mind was too occupied with thoughts of type-sixes and what it meant to be one. There could be little doubt that he was more than human. What opportunities did this present? What drawbacks? What limits were there to his power?

"Did you know that Mr Shadow is supposedly almost 200 years old," he told the headless body of Miss Malice. "How old were you, I wonder. How long will I live?"

He reached up and brushed a finger down the centre of the mask.

All the longer if I can get rid of this.

Aiden had spoken about a nadir, a lowest point at which he was transformed, but Edward could think of no such thing. His life was devoid of traumatic events or abusive parents. He'd been a quiet, studious child. He had a dim recollection of concerns raised about his lack of playing with other children, but that was it. He was normal.

Except...

He had always dreamed about darkness. Its cold tendrils had always been in his heart. What did that mean?

He looked back harder at his life, but the images were hazy and indistinct as always. Edward had never cared much about where he'd come from. He'd always been much more interested in where he was going and what he was going to do to people once he got there.

"Stitches! Get up here."

Edward rolled his eyes. Vasquez was another puzzle. It seemed his claim of immortality was true. Edward knew enough about stabbing people in the neck to know that Miss Malice had dealt Vasquez a deathblow when she'd landed on him. Nevertheless, he was walking around. Edward would need to deal with him sooner or later. Working for Vasquez was a little better than working for the facility.

But how does one kill a dead man?

"Decapitation, perhaps?" he mused as he re-entered the bedroom.

"What?" asked Vasquez.

"Nothing, just daydreaming."

"We're done here," Vasquez collected the papers from Aiden. "We need to rendezvous with the others. It's finally time to put an end to the Mask Program."

"And then I get this mask removed, yes?"

"I haven't forgotten our deal. I'm a man of my word."

"Well, a creature of your word."

Vasquez gave him one of his dead stares, but Edward didn't care.

"What shall we do with the doctor here?" he asked.

Vasquez transferred his corpse-like gaze from Edward to the old man. "He's all yours."

Aiden panicked. "Wait! I gave you what you wanted!"

"I didn't promise you safety. You deserve Hell for what you've done."

Edward stepped forward. "I'm not a religious man, but I'll see what I can do."

"You have no idea what you're doing! The kind of monster you're working with. You have to detonate that mask. He'll kill us all."

Edward grinned. "You know you have excellent teeth. I feel suddenly inspired."

B Y THE TIME EDWARD left the house, he was
covered in blood. He'd placed the doctor's
remains in a neat pile, the teeth arranged into a ring
around them, like mushrooms gleaming white in
the dark. He kept Miss Malice's knives, partly out
of respect and partly because they were pretty little
things and wonderfully sharp.

He hadn't noticed the men surrounding the
house, despite his new and improved senses. An
uncharacteristic error, but he blamed the artistic
urge. They made their presence known as he
stepped out onto the lawn, the torches on their
guns lightning him up in a half circle. Two full
Spectre Teams. No cramped corridors this time.
There was no cover. Edward considered making a
dash back to the house, but he had no desire to be
shot in the back.

There was no sign of Vasquez. Had he given the
doctor to Edward to distract him? It was hard to
say. Did his disappearance mean that the bomb

was no longer protected by the portable deadzone? Could the facility trigger it?

If they could do that, they would have by now. Unless there's some other reason to take me alive.

"Gentlemen," Edward greeted them. He twirled Miss Malice's knives.

Can their guns kill me? Are bullets enough to succeed where the knife failed?

"Stand down, Mr Stitches." Colonel Marsden's voice, projected on loudspeaker. "We're taking you back, whole or in pieces."

"Decisions, decisions."

"I'd prefer in pieces, but the higher ups want you alive. They're going to study you like an animal."

"They've been doing that already." Edward's voice approached a growl. "I'm tired of being a lab rat or a blunt instrument, Colonel."

"You don't have a lot of options, son."

"I could kill you all."

"Take him!" Marsden barked.

In that moment, Edward charged, knives gleaming.

The sound of the guns was a violence unto itself, an assault of thunder. The bullets slammed through him, cleaving flesh and smashing bones. He staggered back under the torrent of lead, his blood misting in the air, his body ripped apart.

They didn't stop until the last gun clicked empty.

"Not a man," Edward told them.

He fell.

Designation: Subject 16

Alias: Mr Eel

Subject Class: Prometheus

Lead Physician: Dr Liebling

Name: Dr Julius Steinman

Date of Birth: 18 October 1949

Acquisition Date: 14 July 1994

Nadir: Mental breakdown due to psychological strain of work with other subjects and subsequent self-experimentation with Prometheus treatments.

Profile: It's clear that Subject 16 considers himself completely sane. A lifetime of medical practice seems to have carried over into his current psychological state, as he has a deep desire to "correct" the perceived ailments of people around him. His delusions lead him to falsely diagnose anyone he comes into contact with and prescribe and carry out extreme treatments, which have no relation to the diagnosis. Before he was captured by staff, the subject managed to perform two lobotomies, several murders via electroshock 'therapy' using cables torn from the wall, and one complete spine removal.

Subject 16 seems unaware that he is incarcerated and seems to believe he is still a lead physician at this facility.

Behavioural Triggers: Subject 16 perceives imagined ailments and a need for immediate medical treatment in all those around him, which he then attempts to provide by nonsensical, erroneous and terribly violent means. His most common 'prescription' is electroshock therapy, for which he shows particular enthusiasm.

Note from Dr Liebling: Dr Steinman was a brilliant man and lead physician on the Mask Program for many years. It saddens us all to see him reduced to this, but in some ways, it can be considered a triumph. Steinman is the first at the facility to successfully become type-six, albeit not under the strictest lab conditions. We can't be fully sure what he did to himself. While he is a viable candidate for Ares classification, study of his physiology and psychology will be crucial to repeating his success under controlled conditions. For this reason, I am recommending he be classified Prometheus.

Note from Dr Steinman: Dr Liebling is clearly suffering from delusions, likely brought on by the stress of perceived competition for the role of lead physician. I assure you that role still belongs to me. I recommend that Liebling be placed into my care for treatment as soon as possible.

Note from Dr Liebling: Can someone please work out how Steinman keeps getting out of his cell and cancel his system login details? This is ridiculous! We are supposed to be a secure facility!

SPARKS AND PRECIOUS DARKNESS

THE DARKNESS WAS SO complete that Edward couldn't tell whether his eyes were open or closed.

The nature of pain had changed for Edward. He understood that it was present, laced through almost every inch of his body, but it didn't incapacitate him as it once would. He registered it more the way he might recognise an itch or a change in temperature. Was this part of being type-six? Another change to his physiology now the lies had begun to fall away?

"I've been pushing for your termination from the start."

Liebling's voice. Fury sparked in Edward, sparking a fire in his core.

The voice had an electronic edge, suggesting that it was coming over a speaker. He knew then that he must be back at the facility. Despite this, he felt that he wasn't restrained. He sought out the bullet holes in his flesh and poked at them. There was no sign of blood or scabbing. Would the wounds close, or was he forced to live forever like Swiss cheese?

He wasn't wearing his clothes, but they'd been shredded by the gunfire, anyway. His mask was disappointingly still in place.

"Despite my many recommendations, you represented too much of a breakthrough for them."

"I'm flattered," said Edward. He probed the edges of the room, arms outstretched, while Liebling rambled on.

"Don't be. It's not to your credit. Steinman was the one who did the work. You're just a lab rat."

"That's the second time I've heard that name today. Assuming it's still the same day, of course."

"Dr Aiden told you about him, I presume. I'd ask you what else you learned from him, but it doesn't matter. You've been reassigned, Edward. No more field trips, no more visits, no more anything. This void is your reality now. Welcome to Persephone."

He wasn't sure whether Liebling could see him, but Edward stopped and forced himself not to panic all the same. He'd always been at home in the dark, but that darkness began to feel oppressive as the idea of being trapped set in. There had to be a way out.

After a few minutes of silence, Edward continued to explore. It was a cell not unlike the one he'd been housed in before, though the door was cleverly hidden, detectable only by the slight air movement at its edges.

Persephone class. The bottom of the facility, where the worst of the worst were housed. Edward wondered who else that roster included. Could he reach them? Should he? His experience with other Masks had been less than favourable thus far, but if he needed a distraction, releasing them would certainly serve that purpose.

Edward didn't waste much time on the door; they wouldn't use one that wasn't secure. He knew Vasquez was bringing the resistance to the facility, but how long would that take? Would they take the place by force or sneak inside? With nothing to do but wait, Edward paced the chamber, learning its size by rote.

The question of his origins as a type-six occupied his thoughts. Liebling had implied that Steinman was somehow responsible. Edward tried to remember his early days at the facility, the circumstances of his arrival, but the memories were dim and distorted, nothing but reflections on turbulent water. His past had been stolen from him along with his present, and someone was going to make it up to him in a particularly bloody fashion.

"Liebling," Edward growled to himself. "Liebling knows."

Edward pictured a thousand ways he could extricate the information if he could just get his hands on the doctor. He was so distracted by his fantasies that he almost didn't hear the voice.

"Hello?"

Edward stopped pacing. Had he imagined it?

"Hello?" A thin sliver of voice through the door.

"Who's there?" Edward called.

"I'll be asking the questions. After all, I'm the doctor here, and you are the patient. What's your name?"

Edward frowned. It wasn't Liebling. "Edward Stitch."

"Ah," the voice gasped. "I've heard so much about you. A very serious case. No wonder they've referred you to me. My name is Dr Steinman. I run this facility."

Over the next few minutes it became very clear that Dr Steinman was completely mad.

"I think we've got a clear case of violent psychosis here, Edward. It's a very serious condition and I suggest we begin treatment right away."

Edward edged closer to the door. Steinman was outside his cell but how could that be? Surely Liebling didn't let a madman go prowling about in the maximum-security wing. "And what treatment would that be?"

"Electroshock therapy is my recommendation. I'll fix you up in no time, don't worry. We'll get that darkness out of you."

"Darkness?"

"I've seen it in many other patients. Mr Monster, Mr Cadaver... why, Mr Shadow is practically dripping in the stuff. It's a real thing. Tangible. Present. The hard part was trying to extract it. A number of subjects didn't survive the process."

Edward leant into the flow of the conversation. "Your work sounds fascinating, doctor."

"We tried blood transfusions and conditioning, various psychotherapies, psychedelics, inducing trauma... we even played with minor brain surgeries! Always looking for that nadir point that Dr Aiden was convinced so of."

"And you found it."

"Oh yes."

"Mr Beast?" Edward guessed.

"Ha, no, no, no! That brute was one of Liebling's guinea pigs. The best he could produce after my own research was shut down. He's after my job, you know? But Mr Beast is marked failure, if you ask me. All the physicality of a type-six but none of the invention or the ingenuity. No perfect darkness, only raw red rage. Still, useful for Ares, I suppose."

"But your work was superior?" Edward pushed the ego button again.

"Naturally. Liebling is bright enough – he's after my job, you know – but he was using damaged goods. No broken soldiers for me. The goal was to take something seen in nature and harness it, not simply recreate it with clumsy prodding. That's why I pushed for healthy test subjects. The board denied me, of course."

Aiden said Steinman had 'lost his marbles'.

"You used yourself."

"Oh yes. And it went spectacularly well, I must say. They locked me up, of course, but they have no idea that they're still my patients. I can leave any time I please, but I choose to stay. I'm the one running this facility. Not Liebling. Me!"

"You can leave your cell?"

"I was here when they put those newer models in. Prometheus was my project."

"Prometheus? Not Persephone?"

"Persephone's a waste of time. Why stick these valuable resources into storage? No, I always pushed for Prometheus. Make them useful, I said! I crept down here to see who the new patient was. I also drop by to see Mr Pogo from time to time. He was my patient too, after all. I have a duty of care."

"Mr Pogo?"

"He used to dress as a clown. One of his many quirks. Acquired him in 1994. Had to fake his execution, of course. Such a shame to have him locked away down here. I could cure him, you know, no matter what they say. I can fix you all."

"And that treatment involves entering this cell?"

"Of course! How else would I attach the cables? You are mad, aren't you?"

Edward considered his options. A locked room or a madman who wanted to electrocute him.

Decisions, decisions.

"Are you able to open the cell, doctor? I think I'd like to proceed with your treatment as soon as possible."

"I seem to have misplaced my keys. Odd... I had a master set before they locked me up. That Liebling, he wants my job."

Edward resisted the urge to bash his head against the door. He collected himself and tried again.

"But my treatment was urgent, remember, doctor? We need to begin right away."

"Yes, it's a very serious case. I recommend electroshock. Ah, here are my cables."

There was the sound of tearing on the other side of the door, like plastic and metal strained beyond limit. A moment later, the door slid aside. The corridor beyond was illuminated only by the frantic sparking of wiring torn from the wall that Dr Steinman held onto. He was a tall, thin individual, a jagged cut of a man, standing as though mid-electrocution himself. The blue-white flickering gleamed from his mask, a pale metal beak with round black lenses for eyes.

"Are you ready to begin?" Steinman asked.

"Begin?" said Edward. "You were going to show me your work, remember? I'm from the board, to approve Prometheus."

Steinman hesitated, looking from Edward to the wire and back. He swayed a little in indecision.

"Unless you'd rather I visit Dr Liebling. I understand his work is quite brilliant."

"Liebling?! No need for that. The young man is quite bright, of course, but he limits himself. Too caught up in morality. Come, let me show you Prometheus. There'll be no doubt who deserves to run the facility then."

"By all means, doctor. Lead on."

Steinman threw the cables away and led the way into the darkness at a brisk walk. Edward could barely make him out in the gloom, even with his heightened vision. Steinman's deeply stained white coat helped, catching the flickering light left behind them. His limbs twitched and jerked occasionally, as though jolted by a charge.

As his eyes adjusted, Edward realised they were passing other cells. Each had a name attached by metal plaque. He reached to trace their names with his fingers. Mr Shape. Mr Collector. Mr Pogo. All entombed in darkness deep beneath the ground.

Such wasted potential.

Edward wondered at their ages, at their crimes. How long had it been since they saw daylight and spilled blood? He wondered what would become of the world if he released them all at once. It was an exciting prospect, but the doors had no visible locks, so there was no way to find out.

For now.

Rather than leading him to a stairwell or elevator, as Edward had expected, Steinman pulled aside a metal panel in the wall and stepped into the darkness beyond. "Hurry along then," he called back. "We shouldn't be seen by the lower personnel. Prometheus is top secret after all. Most don't even know of its existence."

Edward felt his way into the crawlspace only to discover a shaft leading upwards. There was no ladder, but the pipework made it possible, if uncomfortable, to ascend. With little other option, he followed Steinman. His true goal was to find Liebling and extract the truth from him, but he had to admit that Prometheus interested him.

If it gives me a better understanding of what a type-six is capable of, then I want it.

When they emerged several minutes of difficult climbing later, the first thing Edward noticed was the body on the slab.

The room was round, most of the equipment positioned around the gurney at the centre with the exception of a large bank of computers at one side. Several cell doors lined the far side.

"My quarters." Steinman indicated one of the doors. "I find it necessary to keep a room on site. Take it as a sign of my dedication."

Edward approached the body. "Who is this?"

The man was masked, a design intended to look like an executioner's hood over the face, but the cranium behind it was conspicuously absent.

Careful removal of parietal bones had left the brain on display, with all sorts of metal protrusions attached to it.

"This was the first member of Prometheus," said Steinman. "I inherited Mr Cadaver here after Dr Aiden retired. No use for Ares and not dangerous enough for Persephone. As you can see, he's still serving us very well."

"What is this?" Edward leaned down for a better look at the brain. "What are you doing with him?"

"The core of the science! Harnessing the darkness to make type-sixes ourselves. Why wait for messy Mother Nature and her inconsistent rules? We've never understood why a nadir point triggers a transformation in some but not others. Why pan for gold in the chaos when we can simply produce it ourselves? The was where Liebling went wrong with Mr Beast: taking a broken man, pumping him full of darkness and trauma, and hoping for the best."

The body on the slab whispered. "Help me. The dead. I have to stop them."

"Poor man is quite insane, of course," said Steinman. "And, really, not much darkness in him when he came to me. The treatments pushed him further, of course, but other subjects proved far more fruitful."

Steinman moved to one of the doors and rapped on it. Something on the inside started banging immediately, violently. "Steinman! Let me out! I must kill! I must drink the blood!"

"Mr Monster," Steinman said. "Such vigour. Such darkness. I would have liked to get my hands on Mr Pogo and Mr Collector, but I was turned down. My requests to have them transferred to Prometheus were denied. I worked with what I had."

"Yourself."

"As a start, at least. The aim was to use a blank slate."

"Blank?"

"In vitro cultures, of course! Introduce the darkness at the very beginning of life! But I was stopped before I could see that experiment to completion."

"By your incarceration?"

"Do I appear incarcerated to you? Didn't tell you that I'm the lead physician here!"

"Of course, my mistake." Edward pointed to the screens. "And those computers. They contain your research?"

"Mine. Aiden's. The whole lot of it."

"I would very much like to see those records."

E DWARD BARELY NOTICED THE first explosion. His eyes were glued to the screen as he scrolled through. Much of it was password protected and Steinman's access was obviously long revoked. Fortunately, Aiden's access was still good. Edward was glad he questioned the late doctor before removing his teeth. Irritatingly, whilst Aiden's access got him into the bulk of the files, anything that was locked by Liebling was inaccessible, including Edward's.

I will find him before the day is out and have a long, overdue conversation.

Edward gleaned that Prometheus had been Steinman's idea, and Liebling was obliged to pursue it by the board that funded the programme. Whilst Steinman had been obsessed with a quasi-folkloric 'darkness' inside type-sixes and how to extract it, Liebling was more interested in the raw physiology. That was what led to Mr Beast.

But why had Liebling been so insistent on Edward's termination? If it was "right from the start", as the doctor had suggested, it couldn't be personal? The antagonism between them must predate Edward's awareness of it.

The second rumbling caught his attention.

"I believe the resistance has arrived." Edward looked up at the ceiling as though he could see through the concrete. "I'll have words with Vasquez too, when I find him."

Steinman had wandered off, seemingly tired of his own ramblings. Edward had paid little attention to him once the computers were on. He had little understanding of science anyway, and no way to determine fact from madness.

Mr Cadaver remained attached to the slab, brain exposed, occasionally muttering about the living dead. His profile had been uninteresting. Edward was still scrolling back through the other Masks when the main door opened and a Spectre Team entered, guns up.

"Control, we have a Mask loose in the main Prometheus lab," one shouted into his radio. "Please advise."

"You! Get down on the ground, now! Get away from those screens or we will open fire!"

Edward continued to scroll. "You tried that once already. I can't say I enjoyed it much, but it didn't hold me back, either."

"Last warning, freakshow!"

Before Edward could turn and educate the man on his manners, something on the screen made him freeze.

The face staring back at him wasn't his own, but it was so alike that they could be twins.

The name on the profile was Mr Shadow.

DESIGNATION: SUBJECT 18

Alias: Mr Beast

Subject Class: Ares

Lead Physician: Dr Liebling

Name: Brian Jorgensen

Date of Birth: 10 August 1982

Acquisition Date: <REDACTED>

Nadir: Subject was exposed to extreme trauma during military action. Further trauma was introduced as part of the Prometheus treatments.

Profile: Subject has shown extreme physical capabilities including strength, stamina, resistance to injury and pain, and ability to recover from injury.

Subject's mental faculties appear to have been completely overcome by extreme aggression and violent impulse as a result of the Prometheus treatment. Communication with the subject is no longer possible, making psychological evaluation difficult.

Subject reacts with hostility to any human presence, showing a total lack of self-preservation in attempts to attack individuals on sight.

Behavioural Triggers: Attempts to modify subject's behaviour through conditioning have failed. Subject can only be controlled by use of pain as a deterrent. Subject also suffers pyrophobia and will avoid fire where possible. This is the only time when subject shows any emotional other than anger.

Note from Dr Liebling: Despite his unstable nature, Subject 18 should be considered the first successful test of Prometheus treatments since ~~Steinman~~ Subject 16. My recommendation is that we immediately terminate Subject 19 and proceed with Subject 18 as the chief focus of our continued research.

TRUTH UNMASKED

Edward left the Spectre Team in pieces.

Given their surprise, he'd suspected they weren't there for him, but he had never been one to waste an opportunity. He'd done most of it with a scalpel that someone had thoughtfully left out for him. He left that behind but kept the bone saw. He had grand plans for that.

His head was so full of questions that he'd barely paid attention to the killing. With so much of Mr Shadow's information redacted, he was left with only speculation. How could Mr Shadow, a creature almost two hundred years old, have almost his exact likeness? It must have something to do with Liebling's determination to have him killed, but what? Was Edward a descendent with eerily close features?

Liebling knows. Liebling's known the truth all along and he kept it from me. Time for that conversation.

The last thing Edward did before leaving the room was to take a sidearm from one of the bodies, place it carefully against the side of his mask, and pull the trigger. The bullet left his head ringing and his vision swimming, but outcome would be worth it.

Beyond Steinman's room, the facility was made up of plain concrete corridors. As Edward began to stalk his way along them, the facility rocked under the force of another explosion. He had no way of knowing how the resistance's assault was going, and he wondered if Mr Beast was with them, acting as a big, angry battering ram.

He decided against taking the elevator. They'd lock it down as soon as they saw him on the cameras and he couldn't afford the delay; Liebling might make some kind of escape. He pictured the doctor frantically packing bags in his office before sprinting for a helicopter. Edward ran for the stairs. Senses stretched to their limits, he heard the armed men and women before they opened the stairwell door.

"Don't move!" said their leader, shotgun aimed at his head. "We're with De Oppresso Liber!"

Edward reached out, crushed the man's throat, and shoved him into his comrades. "I'm not."

Taking advantage of the confusion, Edward pushed his way into their midst, seizing the next one by the head and twisting it in a way that necks should not be twisted. In the next heartbeat Edward seized a fire axe from the wall and carried out a smooth decapitation of one unfortunate woman, before burying it in the chest of another. The final woman backed up and fired. A spray of bullets cut through Edward's abdomen.

"There was a time when that would have irritated me." He pulled the axe free with a spray of gore. He stalked closer, naked, bloody and masked, a nightmare image of murder. "I would like to talk to Vasquez, please."

VASQUEZ'S VOICE CAME THROUGH in his recognizable dead tones over the communications device. "Our distraction is done. Mr Beast breached the main entrance, but they shot him to hell. Bits of him are still moving, but I'm not sure he's getting back up."

"That's a shame," Edward spoke into the radio. "He had potential."

"Stitches?"

"Hello, Vasquez. You left me to be captured."

"Or killed. Am I supposed to feel sorry?"

"I thought you were a man of your word."

"I'm not a man. You said so yourself."

"Then I guess we'll find out who the greater monster is."

"Maybe. But when push comes to shove, would you rather kill me or these people?"

"Your sales pitch needs updating. I'm far stronger than I was. I'm reasonably confident I can kill all of you."

"Don't kid yourself. Either side has enough firepower to end you, type-six or not."

"Not you, though. The portable deadzone was a lie, wasn't it? You never had the ability to detonate my mask, or you would have done it when you left me at Aiden's."

"Worked, didn't it? I knew they wouldn't blow you up unless they had to."

"I don't like liars. Or leashes."

Edward dropped the radio on the body and left it there. He whistled to himself as he headed down the corridor.

As he listened to his footsteps, he smiled. He'd never seen this corridor, but he knew it regardless. The floor was as familiar to him as the weight of his mask. This was his corridor. His cell was here. That meant the other Ares class cells might also be here.

A little firepower of my own. A little extra chaos. And if a few make it out into the world, well, the world will be much more interesting.

Much like the cells of Persephone class, there were no visible means of opening the doors, so

Edward drew the conclusion that they must be opened remotely.

"Welcome home, Edward. I see you didn't like your new room. I don't know how you got out, but you should have stayed put."

It was Liebling over the speaker system. He hadn't run for his helicopter yet.

"I assume you were the one inside the Prometheus lab. I see that files were accessed from there, and the Spectre Team sent to investigate has gone offline. What did you learn, Edward? You're still missing answers, aren't you? Don't you realise this is futile, Edward? You've been playing our game from the start, and you didn't even know it."

Edward passed cell after cell, most of them nameless. Miss Malice and Mr Beast still had theirs.

"Every step you take is by design. You think Vasquez is with the resistance? A type-six just walking around outside of our control? He was a plant. We're playing the same game we've been playing your whole life, even before we put that mask on you. You belong to us, Edward. You always did, ever since you were born."

Edward marched faster.

"Go back to your cell, Edward. You've passed our tests with flying colours. We're ready to discuss a promotion. Better quarters, a few luxuries. As soon as this ruckus is dealt with, it'll be time for your reward."

Even over the speakers, Edward could hear his desperation. The only way to the truth was to get Liebling alone in person. As Edward rounded a corner he spotted the guard station with two guards in attendance that he recognised.

Edward smiled.

What a wonderful opportunity.

Thing One looked up just in time to see the whirling axe crashed through the window of the station and cleaved his skull in half. His body flew backwards off its chair and landed in a bloody heap on the floor. Thing Two screamed in anger, bursting through the doorway with his taser drawn. Edward stepped up and slashed his fingers with the bone saw before he could pull the trigger. While Thing Two screamed, his bloody fingers rolling across the floor, Edward dragged the saw across the stocky guard's stomach. Each stroke sprayed Edward with warm blood and gore.

Thing Two fell to his knees, pale and panting in shock, while bits of him started to slide out from their proper homes. Delicately, Edward ran a hand through the guard's hair, and then gripped it and yanked his head back, exposing his neck.

"I bet thirty-two," Edward whispered to him.

In the end it took thirty-eight strokes to remove the head, but Edward wasn't sore about it. Instead, he basked in the catharsis of years of anticipation fulfilled as he examined the control panel. Since none of the buttons were labelled, he pressed them all. Immediately a blaring alarm and lots of flashing lights started up. Satisfied, Edward left the shack, bowled Thing Two's head underarm down the corridor, then went through the newly unlocked door beside the station.

The control room where Marsden had briefed him was down a set of concrete steps. Gunfire echoed somewhere ahead and, beneath that thunderous sound, screaming. He found a new corridor littered with bodies of both Spectres and resistance fighters. He forced himself not to skip across them.

The gunfire died down ahead of him and he heard voices. Marsden's drawl was easily identifiable. "You don't know what you're doing, son."

There was pain in each word. Marsden was clearly wounded.

"I'm bringing this place down." Vasquez's dead tones.

"You're one of them."

"So?"

"What's going to happen to you out in the world? You need the research we're doing here."

"And you're going to hand that over?"

Edward stepped into the room. "I'll tell you where it is. But there's several loose Ares class between you and it by now."

The control room, formerly so orderly and clean, was a ruin of broken equipment, bleeding bodies, and bullet holes. Marsden was collapsed against a desk, one hand clutching a gut wound while the other aimed a wavering gun at Vasquez. The sweat of pain was on his brow, and he bared his teeth as he recognised Edward.

Vasquez held some kind of assault rifle, though it wasn't pointed at Marsden. Instead, his attention was on rucksack of explosives he'd evidentially been carrying. He took Edward in with his usual level of dispassion.

"Where might I find Dr Liebling?" Edward asked. "I have questions."

Marsden ignored his question. "You let them out? The Ares class are loose?"

"Oh yes. They'll be along soon, depending on which way they go."

"Damn," Vasquez growled. He returning to unpacking the explosives.

Marsden squeezed the trigger and blew a chunk of Vasquez' skull away. Vasquez ignored it.

"Don't you want that research? I thought that was your driving motivation." Edward was genuinely curious.

Vasquez didn't look up. "I became a soldier to protect people. If you think I'm going to choose finding my own answers over keeping those things from escaping, you've got the wrong idea of me."

"We don't need to bring this place down for that." Marsden hauled himself up and towards a control panel. "Just detonate their masks."

"Lies are bad for you, Colonel," said Edward. "Ares class, at least, have their masks removed in their cells."

"That still leaves Persephone and all the others. And you've still got yours. That's a start." Marsden lifted a cover and flipped the switch beneath it.

Nothing.

Edward tilted his face to one side and pointed to the dent in the side of his mask. "Sorry. The receiver on Mr Beast's bomb was knocked out by a similar shot, so I took inspiration from that. You should have blown me up when you could." Slowly, Edward reached up and removed the mask, letting it drop to the floor.

"I should have."

"Why didn't you?"

"Orders. Detonating a Mask is a last resort. Type-sixes are too rare, especially compliant ones. But Liebling always said you were too much of a risk."

"Broken clocks and all that. Where is he?"

"I'm sure as Hell not telling you."

"I'll convince you." Edward raised the bone saw and inspected the bloody teeth. "I'm feeling creative."

Marsden met his gaze. Then, eyes hardened, he put the gun to his own head and pulled the trigger. The gunshot echoed loud in the wreck of the command centre.

"Well," said Edward. "That was dramatic."

He turned to Vasquez, who regarded him, detonator in hand.

Edward heard movement in the corridor behind him over the alarm. Footsteps, the scraping of a blade against something hard, a faint lullaby hummed discordantly. The rest of Ares. Would they be allies, or rabid dogs like Mr Beast? Perhaps they'd just rip each other to shreds.

"What will it be, Mr Stitches?" Vasquez asked. "Are you going to face the end like a man?"

"I am not a man."

Time seemed to slow for Edward. He saw the dead man's muscles moving, tendons tightening to pull the trigger.

Cold white fingers seized Edward's shoulder in an iron grip. Then he was hurtling backwards down the corridor as though he weighed no more than a stuffed toy. Before he hit the ground, a flash of light went off and, for a moment, a ragged silhouette stood in the glow. A tall, thin man, shadows wreathed around him, his face turned to the side. In that thinly sliced portion of a second, Edward knew Mr Shadow was looking at him.

The shockwave of the blast hit Edward and flung him violently down the corridor. He collided with the wall, twisted and tumbled, crashed into the ceiling, spun about, and rolled in chaos until he didn't know which way was up. All along the tumultuous journey, the roar of the explosion chased him. When he hit the back wall, it crashed against him like a furious wave and ripped the light right out of his eyes.

WHEN EDWARD CAME TO, bits of the ceiling were still falling.

The roar of the explosion had given way to a constant rumbling as the bones of the facility started to fail. The corridor to the control centre had collapsed entirely. The only exit was the stairway he'd taken to this floor.

He hauled himself up, head ringing. He had broken bones and gained fresh lesions to add to his collection of wounds. He felt his ribs grinding against each other in shards. The white curve of them was visible in places where his skin had been shredded away. A splinter of his own thigh bone sawed into the meat of his leg with each step. He analysed these things coldly. Pain was a distant thing, a polite advisory rather than a brutal seizure of the senses.

Had Mr Shadow saved him? Or had he simply hauled Edward out of his way? Edward was certain some recognition had passed between them. There was a connection there. But what?

Liebling knows.

Edward staggered to the stairwell and started to climb.

Edward only made it three flights up before he was greeted by a large hole in the wall overlooking the cavernous hanger. It pleased him to see helicopters already crushed or on fire. There would be no escape.

Looking down on the chaos he saw facility staff running in every direction. He saw some splattered as debris fell on them. He watched a group in lab coats run from a man whose mask was made-up like a clown. Even from that distance, Edward heard him ask, "Want to see a magic trick?"

He saw another Mask, though not for long enough to identify them, try to pull the metal from their face. The detonation added to the chaos.

Edward turned away and moved on up the staircase as though in a dream. For so long he'd wanted to see the facility fall. For so long he'd wanted to be free of the mask. It was everything he'd hoped for. Everything was right with the world.

There was only one thing missing. He needed those answers. Who was he? How long had the Program been manipulating him?

Soon. I'll know soon.

A section of the stairs collapsed and a blast of cold air almost flattened him. He turned to see the open sky and, beneath it, mountains and forest as far as the eye could see. The facility was built directly into a mountain that was, it seemed, collapsing.

Edward could leave through that hole. He would survive the forest, the wilderness, and the cold. He would make it back to civilisation. The door to freedom was directly in front of him. No mask. No bomb. A world of possibility.

He was caught in indecision, between escape and ignorance. The facility could collapse any minute. He wasn't sure he would survive if he was still inside, even with his new abilities. Worse than death, he could be trapped forever under thousands of tonnes of rock, imprisoned again but without any reprieve.

I have to know. And Liebling must pay.

T HE TOP LEVEL OF the facility was a nicely carpeted office corridor. Wooden doors faced each other across it, each with a name beside it. Great splits had cracked the wood-panelled walls, and Edward heard the them groaning under growing pressure. He didn't have long.

Liebling's office was at the end.

It was clear he'd been trying to escape. The office was ransacked, notes and papers scattered about. A metal case lay just out of reach where he'd fallen. He was trapped beneath a fallen bookcase, pinned from the waist down but very much alive.

His face turned grey when he saw Edward.

"Hello, doctor. I believe we have an appointment."

Liebling was caught between seething hatred and utter fear.

"I have questions," Edward said. "You have answers."

"Kill me and you'll never know them. I'll tell you a dozen truths before I die. You'll never know which one is real. You were an orphaned child we took in and experimented on, implanting false memories of a boring childhood. You're a mundane killer with delusions of being an unstoppable monster. You're still locked up, even now. Nothing you perceive is real."

"Stop. This won't save you. As you know, I like to use an implement of some kind to work with. A tool. With you, I think I'll use my hands."

The facility shook again. Lights flickered. Something in the corridor shattered.

"Get me out!" Liebling cried. "I'll tell you everything! The truth!"

Edward crouched and flexed his fingers. "But as you said, I'll never know which one is real. You're a convincing liar, after all."

Liebling raised his hands for mercy. "You're a clone! Steinman grew you in a lab! I wanted you destroyed when we found you, but the board decided to try an old catch-and-release proposal of Aiden's to see what would happen!"

"A clone of Mr Shadow?"

"Amongst others. Your genetic profile is varied. Steinman's perfect monster. You never gazed into the abyss, Edward. You never had a nadir. The abyss was in you all along."

"You appeal to my ego, doctor. I remember a childhood. There's a lack of glowing vats and science labs in those memories."

"Implanting a false memory is easy. How much detail do you remember? What specifics? Are you recalling images or just information? If we can convince a monster that they're a man, what else can we convince you of?"

Edward paused. The building rumbled again. Bits of the office ceiling crumbled, and dust rained down. He could still make it to the hole in the stairs. He knew he was fast enough.

"Save me and I'll tell you everything," Liebling pleaded.

"You kept me captive. You lied to me. You diminished me, humiliated me, brainwashed and taunted me." He leaned down, face close Liebling's. "And you were very rude."

Parts of the ceiling fell in behind them. The floor bucked and the mountain groaned.

"Please! You'll never know who you really are!"

Each possibility the doctor presented in his desperate tirade of lies pushed Edward towards a different truth. There were glaring unknowns in his past, it was true, but what did that change? No amount of testing, torture or incarceration had changed him thus far. He was who he was. That was his truth.

Edward leaned down and looked Liebling in the eye.

"I am Mr Stitches. That's truth enough for me."

As the facility collapsed around them, Edward lunged.

THE END

DESIGNATION: SUBJECT 2

Alias: Miss Lullaby

Subject Class: Ares

Lead Physician: Dr Aiden

Name: Unknown

Date of Birth: Unknown. Estimated early 1900s

Acquisition Date: 7 July 1959

Nadir: Speculated to be the death of/abandonment by subject's mother and subsequent isolation in the woods for years.

Profile: The subject was discovered in a densely forested area around Chernobyl after an investigation of local legends. These legends refer to the subject as a "Bear Woman", "Bodark", or "Werewolf", and say that those who venture deep into the woods might hear her "lullaby". This folklore suggests that the subject has been active in this area since at least World War I, as the disappearance of German troops in the area during 'the fall of the Empire' is referred to in some local stories and attributed to the subject.

The subject was discovered to be occupying a dwelling deep within the forest. The house was decorated with multiple hunting trophies including the skulls of bears, elk, and wolves. Some had been made into masks or headdresses. Curiously, the subject also appeared to have made or gathered various simple toys, and displayed a family portrait on the wall. The toys were gathered in one corner, where ropes and chains were also present.

The subject shows extraordinary strength and resilience and was able to fatally wound many personnel before finally succumbing to sedation.

The subject hums a particular lullaby, a Russian folk song, ceaselessly. The subject seems to require no food or sleep. The subject does not talk but appears to understand simple instructions, though is largely non-compliant.

Behavioural Triggers: The subject will violently attack at any opportunity but seems to have a particular preference for giving chase to fleeing victims. Coupled with the display of trophies at her "home", it can be speculated that she enjoys hunting, and sees no difference between people and prey.

The subject refuses weapons except axes and hatches, though she will use her bare hands if these are denied. The subject is a fine candidate for Ares Classification, as she will kill any targets in a designated area hunt any who attempt to escape. However, note that the subject will not harm children. Instead, she attempts to take them captive, especially young girls. Avoid deployments which include children in the target pool.

DESIGNATION: SUBJECT 3

Alias: Mr Shape

Subject Class: Persephone

Lead Physician: Dr Aiden (formerly Dr <REDACTED>).

Name: <REDACTED>

Date of Birth: Unknown, estimated 1957

Acquisition Date: ~~1963, 1978, 1989,~~ 2018

Nadir: Unknown

Profile: The subject refuses to speak, no matter the coercion used, so full psychological analysis is difficult. The subject first killed at age 6, without any evidence of a motivation, psychological or otherwise. After much study, the diagnosis of Dr <REDACTED> was that the subject is 'purely and simply evil'. Dr <REDACTED> was removed as lead physician for Subject 3 shortly afterward and placed on indefinite leave out of concerns for his mental health.

The subject seems to form an obsession with one particular individual. The subject will kill, often with spectacular violence, anyone between him and the object of this obsession.

The subject escaped <REDACTED> Sanatorium several times before being transferred to the current facility.

Behavioural Triggers: The subject spends much of his time in a comatose state but seems to 'awaken' every October 31st. This occurs regardless of efforts to prevent the subject from having knowledge of the date. Increase lockdown measures for the subject on October 31st.

The subject has shown a preference for a chef's knife as their primary tool.

Note from Dr Aiden: Subject 7 is perhaps the clearest case of a human being becoming a type-six entity. His physical abilities, particularly resistance to physical harm and to the aging process, have gradually transcended human capability with each new escape and killing spree. My repeated recommendations for a "catch and release" protocol to measure this increase have been denied.

Designation: Subject 11

Alias: Mr Cadaver

Subject Class: Prometheus

Lead Physician: Dr Aiden

Name: Julian Ketch

Date of Birth: 1 June 1951

Acquisition Date: 18 April 1978

Nadir: Death of mother

Profile: The subject experiences delusions and hallucinations that cause him to believe people around him are 'the living dead'. The subject appears to perceive wounds on these individuals, which he refers to as 'death-wounds'. He believes these 'death-wounds' show him how to kill the living dead, which he is then compelled to do.

The subject is generally cooperative and personable unless his delusions are challenged, after which he becomes agitated.

Behavioural Triggers: There seems to be no discernible pattern to the subject's victims. He cannot be given specific targets, which makes him unsuitable for Ares class.

Note from Dr Steinman: Subject 11 is the perfect candidate for my proposed Prometheus class: he has no further use in study and cannot be deployed into the field as Ares class. I know Dr Aiden resisted this proposal, but I would like to remind the board that Dr Aiden is no longer the lead physician on the project. Prometheus is the natural next step in the programme.

DESIGNATION: SUBJECT 14

Alias: Mr Pogo

Subject Class: Persephone

Lead Physician: Dr Steinman

Name: <REDACTED>

Date of Birth: <REDACTED>

Acquisition Date: 10 May 1994

Nadir: Childhood abuse.

Profile: Subject 14 appears to have had an extremely traumatic childhood, leading to a deeply repressed sexuality and subsequent abuse by the subject to his victims.

The subject often tricked victims into tying themselves up with handcuffs on the pretence of displaying "a magic trick", before subjecting them to torture. The subject often subjected victims to verbal taunting throughout.

The subject's obsession with dressing as a clown appears to be an attempt to revert to a 'safe' childhood state. This state of 'clowning' often lasts until the subject experiences sexual arousal, at which point their murderous intent surfaces.

Behavioural Triggers: The subject's preferred method of execution is the "rope trick": strangulation via an improvised tourniquet tightened around the neck.

If the subject asks, at any point, to show personnel a "magic trick" or uses any wording similar to this, personnel are to IMMEDIATELY enact lockdown protocol 3-alpha.

Note from Dr Aiden: Since Dr Steinman's "treatments", Subject 14 has become far more vicious and powerful. It seems that Steinman was attempting to locate a biological component of type-six transformation by intentionally exacerbating the subject's mental state. Given Dr Steinman's current condition, it seems unlikely this approach was based on any scientific methodology.

DESIGNATION: SUBJECT 15

Alias: Mr Collector

Subject Class: Persephone

Lead Physician: Dr Aiden

Name: <REDACTED>

Date of Birth: 21 May 1960

Acquisition Date: 28 Nov 1994

Nadir: Unknown

Profile: The subject has been diagnosed with various psychotic disorders, including schizotypal personality disorder.

The subject shows intense psychosexual confusion. Sexual fantasies experienced by subject typically involve dismemberment, dissection and/or cannibalism. The subject has also engaged in necrophilia.

The subject has an interest in the preservation of his victims, typically their bones. Interviews with the subject suggest that this practice is a form of reverence for the victims that he was particularly attracted to.

The sexual urge in the subject has been conflated with desire to murder. Murder has replaced the act of sexual intercourse.

Behavioural Triggers: The subject shows a fascination for the male body, with a particular focus on the chest and torso area. The subject is particularly intent on the murder of those men he is sexually attracted to. Attempts to utilise this to control the subject have failed, often fatally. Recommend the subject be reclassified to Persephone.

Designation: Subject 19

Alias: Mr Stitches

Subject Class: Ares

Lead Physician: Dr Liebling

Name: Edward Stitch

Date of Birth: <REDACTED>

Acquisition Date: <REDACTED>

Nadir: <REDACTED>

Profile: <REDACTED>

Behavioural Triggers: <REDACTED>

ABOUT THE AUTHOR
Jim Horlock

Jim Horlock lives in Cardiff, Wales, where he writes weird stories and collects ghosts. He's a huge nerd, a boardgamer, a dungeon master, and a cryptid enthusiast. You can find his stories in anthologies from Eerie River Publishing, Endless Ink Press, and on podcasts such as CreepyPod and NoSleep. A book of his short horror stories, CHANGES, was released from Quill & Crow Publishing House Summer of 2024.

Printed in Great Britain
by Amazon